THE KEEPERS

REUTS PUBLICATIONS

THE *Keepers*

ANOOSHA LALANI

Cover design by Ashley Ruggirello
Cover art Copyright 2014 Desert-Winds/lillyfly06-stock on DeviantArt.com

ISBN: 978-1-942111-03-0

REUTS Publications
www.REUTS.com

To Inara,

For being the thread to my needle as I stitched up plot hole after plot hole.

Prologue

usk; the hour between evening and night. Darkness was descending upon the frenzied market—a vulture prepared to envelop the Earth under its shadowy wings. Women held their purses close, and men hurried to sell their final products. Pickpockets trailed after careless customers, stealing anything they could get their hands on to afford tomorrow's meal. Shop stalls had already begun to light up with lanterns, oil lamps, and hanging light bulbs, warding away the threat of nightfall. Their gaudy glow attracted mosquitoes and other insects with beating wings. A melody of sharp buzzing could be clearly heard.

A shopkeeper felt a feathery touch as one landed on the base of his wrist. A river of blood and temptation had caught the eye of the small insect. Agitated, Mikal swatted it away with the grace and speed of a predatory cat.

Getting back to work, he grunted as he lifted the elegant mahogany table from his donkey-drawn cart. His muscles tensed beneath the sweat-stained grey of his shirt. He did this every day, yet it never got any easier. In fact, he was getting older, and his strength was beginning to leave him. He balanced the weight of the table precariously between his arms, so carefully; his knuckles were white from the pressure, and his face twisted in concentration. His knees shook violently. He couldn't drop this piece. It had taken him weeks to complete. The crisscrossing carpenter's cuts patterned on the tapestry of his arms were a reminder of the many hours spent in his workshop.

If this sold well, his family would have rice for a day. Fluffy, white, soft grains of rice. His tongue automatically licked his chapped lower lip. Rice had become an expensive commodity—one his family could no longer afford. Instead, they had learned to survive on the plain *chapattis* that his wife so fondly kneaded.

A shrill whirr, louder than any insect he had ever heard before, awoke him from his reverie. A single muscle in his neck twitched as he turned. Immediately, his eyes focused on the pests flying directly above his head.

"*Bhai Saab!*"

Hearing the yell, Mikal quickly looked away from the insects and observed his company. He had come face to face with a soldier—a young one, almost twenty years his junior and little older than a teenager, dressed in black combat boots and the trademark camouflage uniform.

"Watch where you step!" the soldier hollered.

Mikal nodded, his arms shaking slightly as they grew tired of the table's weight. He waited for a dismissal.

"Go on! Move along!" the soldier bellowed.

Mikal rushed past him, his elbow brushing the soldier's. The soldier's elbow melted from his touch. No longer solid, it was a limb of nothingness. Before Mikal could process what he had seen, the buzzing was back and with it, the insects.

They flew out of the soldier from every visible orifice: eyes, ears, mouth, nose. Skin and clothes shredded, the soldier transformed into a hideous wave of black. Thousands of beetle-like creatures now occupied the space where the soldier stood just seconds ago. A few of them landed upon Mikal's arms. He twitched, blinking his eyes quickly, and staggered back, the weight of the table throwing him off balance. He tried to increase the distance between him and the swarming beasts, but the bugs came closer still.

They were so close that Mikal could see the limbs connected to the creatures' black-winged bodies. Arms, hands, legs, feet. Embedded in their long white faces were lips so red they looked like they had been stained with blood.

The corners of one creature's mouth lifted in an unkind smile, revealing pointed, snowy fangs. It bit down into Mikal's sinewy flesh, sinking its incisors deep into the wound it had created.

He jerked in agony and the table crashed onto his feet with a crunch, crushing his tiny toe bones. His arms flailed wildly in a futile attempt to smack the creatures off his skin, and as he did so, he fell back, hitting his head hard on the ground. Sharp bursts of pain erupted all over his body as more of the airborne creatures landed upon him. A flow of warm blood coated Mikal's arm.

He struggled to sit up, paralyzed with fear. His eyes were wide as a creature leapt up to his face and slit his eyeballs out in one quick, angry motion. Licking the milky globe in its pale hand, it giggled with odious pleasure while the poor shopkeeper writhed on the floor—a worm trapped in a tube with no end.

Tears of blood fell from Mikal's empty sockets, crusting his face scarlet. He opened his mouth and another creature dove straight into it, stifling what would have been a terrifying scream. It clawed at his throat and slashed at his insides. He coughed bloody phlegm.

Finally, Mikal shut his empty eyelids. He clung to the memories of his two young daughters and his beautiful wife. They would be the last people he saw before death claimed him. Peacefully lost in thought, his lungs compressed and his last breath of air left him. A soulless carcass was left in his place.

One

Isra

The hunger cramps gnawed at my empty stomach. They crept into the hollow insides of my body, silent and sly, snatching the sleep I had only just fallen into. I fooled the yearning for a while by wrapping a cloth tight around my torso. I almost convinced myself that I wasn't hungry. *Almost.* Now, enraged at the deception, the hunger was back with a vengeance. It was useless to try to go back to sleep. I had worn out my welcome in the dreamers' lands.

I glanced at the silhouette of Zaffirah, lying beside me. The blanket, having slipped off her skinny body, now lay in an untidy heap on the floor. I picked it up and gently pulled it over her cold shoulders. She rolled, spinning a cocoon in its wool, and sighed happily. I felt my lips part in a smile that echoed her short-lived contentment.

Sparing a final glance at my sister, I crept out of the one-room house. The door wailed behind me as its rusted hinges creaked. I hoped silently that it hadn't woken my sister and began walking along the dirt road. I moved past rows of corrugated iron and wooden shacks toward the only well in our slum. Maybe I could fill my stomach with water instead. I had done it before on many occasions.

I looked back. From a distance, my home looked like a human bird's nest, but they all did. Every broken house in every filthy slum in Islamabad—if they could even be called houses. The crumbling infrastructure was the framework of my life.

I continued walking, and within seconds, I was greeted with the smell of excretion and vomit. I pulled my gauzy *dupatta* over my nose, but the stench permeated the thin fabric. My breath automatically turned shallow as my feet pulled me forward, further into the slum. The tiny rocks of sand bounced off my slipper-encased feet and grains found their way into my shoes and between my toes.

My stomach groaned violently, a reminder that it was still waiting to be fed. I stopped beside the faded brick well.

A sixteen-year-old girl with dark, tangled locks, thinly layered with grime, looked back at me from the well's deep, dark depths. My fingers automatically combed my hair, undoing the knots with little success. Knowing the hopelessness of the task I had taken on, I dropped my hands to the metal pail and pushed it into the well, causing ripples that distorted my reflection. When I pulled the pail back out, it was overflowing, unable to contain the water. I cupped my hands together to sip the cool liquid it held. The water ran down my throat, feeding every inch of my body. It soothed my stomach for less than a second before the ache of starvation was back.

I refilled the empty pail and lifted it to my head, the palms of my hands carefully supporting its weight as I turned, ready to make my way back home.

"*Abbeh*!" The sharp voice snapped me out of my thoughts.

Meters ahead, two boys were yelling at each other. "You have three seconds to give it to me!"

I knew that voice. It was Farid, the fisherman's son and, occasionally, my friend.

"Or what?" the other boy asked, smirking.

Farid held up one finger. Then he brought up the second. Just as quickly as the third appeared, he punched the boy across the jaw. Red globules of saliva flew from the boy's mouth to the ground. Farid's temper rose like the howls of wind, unexpectedly and often with harsh cruelty. The very rage he displayed now. His face was twisted into a mask of grotesque fury. He wasn't done. He straightened his leg and kicked the boy in the gut.

The boy fell to the ground, clutching his stomach. Farid then bent down and whispered something into the boy's ear before snatching a white plastic bag out of his clutches.

"Farid, stop!" I ran toward them. The water from my pail spilled in large droplets down my face, hanging off the tips of my eyelashes and fusing with the sweat on my cheeks. Farid didn't so much as glance in my direction. His head lolled back, and he stared, expressionless, at the vast expanse of the sky. I glared at him—a futile gesture since I knew he wouldn't notice—before putting down my pail and turning to the boy, who was still curled up on the ground in a fetal position.

"Can you stand?" I asked the boy. When he nodded, I helped him to his feet. His eyelid was purple, swollen to the size of my fist from the blow. He could hardly look at me. His face was a wreck, stained with blood and tears.

"Do you need me to help you get home?" I asked, though I knew the moment the question slipped from my lips that he would say *no*. I regretted asking it.

The boy shook his head and wiped fiercely at his tears. "Don't touch me!" he snapped.

Without another word, he hobbled away, leaning on his right leg. I stared at him until he disappeared from my line of sight. Then I turned to Farid, not even bothering to ask him why.

He didn't give me the chance to, anyway. He broke out into a crooked grin. "That boy seemed awfully eager to get away from his darling savior, didn't he?"

I ignored his words and instead scanned him, head to toe. He hadn't suffered a single injury. Just as I'd expected. He had been in so many fights, there weren't many that could lay a finger upon him anymore. His skin was unmarked, unlike the other boys, who carried their scars like trophies; his unblemished skin marked his victory over all of them. Few dared to a pick a fight with him, but that didn't decrease the number of fights he got into anyway. That boy was brave, fighting Farid. Brave, but stupid.

I walked away from Farid. He didn't bother to stop me.

It was about time I got home. My mother would be getting up soon, and she would wonder where I was. I picked up the pail and took the shortcut, wandering away from the main path and into the labyrinth of narrow, congested alleyways. Furry mice scuttled away as they heard the sound of my human footsteps. I stepped past the assortment of trash that decorated the area. The rats had taken refuge in the empty metal cans.

"*Sssss.*"

I stopped. My ears pricked at the hissing. It was a sound that could only come from the forked tongue of a snake.

"*Isssrraaa.*"

A snake that could speak.

I had heard the snake-like voice call my name many times in the past few weeks. At first, I thought it was insects, but now, I knew better. The snake had visited me in my dreams too; I had seen it. It had eyes like dark, infinite oceans, and it would come closer and closer till I woke up, breathing heavy, in a pool of my own sweat. I jerked away instinctively, trying to find my way out of the alleys. The shortcut was a mistake.

I quickened my pace, but the voice surrounded me. In whichever direction I went, it got louder and louder. Every step I took brought me closer to its owner.

"*Isssrraaaa.*"

I closed my eyes and ran. My heart thumped, beating raggedly against my chest.

"*Ooof.*" I opened my eyes to see what I had knocked into. The hissing was gone. A dark grey creature about three feet high stood before me. His skin was made entirely of stone, and he looked almost like a grumpy cat standing on its hind legs. Certainly not human, but not animal either. A creature of a completely different race altogether—one not from this world. I let out the sigh of relief I hadn't realized I was holding in. Anything was better than the snake.

"Dearg! Where have you been? I missed you," I moaned. I put the almost-empty pail down and cradled the heavy creature in my arms. He put his thick arms around my neck, holding tight.

"Miss you too!" he croaked. "Got stuffs to tell you—"

Tap Tap Tap. Footsteps. Settling Dearg carefully on his webbed feet beside me, I brought a finger to my lips, gesturing for him to be quiet. I looked up to see Farid sauntering toward me.

"Couldn't help following me, could you?" I murmured, my voice dripping sarcasm. I couldn't be sure that he had heard me.

His green gaze penetrated me, devoid of emotion. Not many people in our slum had eyes as green as his. It was rare amongst our people. There were rumors that his mother was a devil-worshiping witch. I had known Farid his whole life, but the woman had barely spoken more than a few words to me.

"Are you stalking me now?" I asked, raising my eyebrows.

"You are so terribly hard to resist." A mocking light danced in his eyes. "I heard you talking to someone, and you have a total of one friend. Me." He eyed me, a grin playing on his lips again. "I was curious. Is it a crime to be curious?"

"I wasn't talking to anyone." The words left my mouth quickly.

As subtly as I could, I pushed Dearg behind me, though I knew Farid wouldn't be able to see him anyway. He turned inquisitively toward where Dearg had stood at my side, but he rubbed his eyes and quickly returned his gaze to my face again. *He would have seen an empty space beside me, nothing more,* I told myself.

"Okay. Whatever you say," he replied, his shoulders relaxing.

I softened my voice and changed the subject. "Farid, why did you hurt him?"

"Who? That boy? I taught him a lesson. He deserved what he got."

"Yes, I'm sure he did. Like the one last week?"

He shrugged before opening his mouth. "He should be glad I didn't slit his throat. I'm not going to make you believe me. Friends usually have this thing called trust."

"Since when are we friends?" I replied. He didn't respond. I watched his face fall. His eyes turned dark. Farid's emotions always had a way of creeping onto the features of his face. His beautiful, high-cheekboned face. It was a face so angelic that it almost masked the intensity of his temper. Guilt washed over me. I sighed. "Farid, I'm sorry, but you have to stop. You hurt that boy badly, and he wasn't the only one you've hurt."

I scooped up the pail as the last droplets of water dribbled out.

"Your pail is empty. You should be more careful with that thing." His voice had softened. It had a magnetism that I couldn't explain. Kind, it was not, but maybe, it could have passed for thoughtful. I nodded and pushed Dearg forward, looking back every few minutes to make sure Farid wasn't trailing behind us. When I was sure we were safely alone, I stopped.

"Dearg, what were you saying?" I asked.

"Isra papa in trouble," he grumbled.

"What? Dearg, what happened to him?"

"Can't say. Isra must ask Mama," he murmured. I grabbed the creature by his shoulders and shook him hard. My nails would have cut through his skin if it were not solid stone. Despite this, his expression didn't change.

"Tell me. Now!" I demanded.

"Can't say," he repeated.

Poof. The creature disappeared, leaving iridescent wisps of smoke in his place. He had a habit of doing that at precisely the most annoying of moments. Regardless, a strange trust had developed between us, and I knew he wasn't lying.

Racing home, I crashed through the door, instantly spotting my mother sitting on the ground with her head in her hands. I heard her sharp intakes of air. My sister entered the room with a crumpled, plastic cup of water. She placed it on the floor across from my mother. I could see the wet trails of tears on her cheeks, but she said nothing.

"Zaffirah . . . ?" I probed.

In answer, she picked up the torn newspaper on the ground, smoothed it out, and held it to me. I took it from her hands and peered at the front page. It was dated almost five days ago.

"*Market . . . er . . . er . . . erupts with the k . . . kh . . . chaos of fight . . . fighting sold . . . soldiers,*" I struggled to read out loud. My mother had taught me the letters, but I still had trouble with the words. "Papa," I said with shock, when the meaning of the article finally registered. My heartbeat grew louder in my ears. All I could hear was its rhythmic beat. My sister's lips moved, but I heard nothing. I didn't want to hear any more.

Two

Isra

One Week Earlier

My hands worked, almost mechanically, wetting the wooden crate that we used as our table and then wiping it dry. There was hardly anything on the table to clean off. No crumbs, no drops. We were careful with our food, having so little of it, but my mother insisted that the crate be wiped anyway, as always.

My father made beautiful furniture. I'd seen each and every single one of his tables and chairs. None of which we ever used ourselves. It was furniture that he sold to bring food to our wooden crate. He had just finished making this beautiful brown table, and on the legs, he had carved huge horses leaping over nonexistent cliffs. That was the table he was going to sell today at the market.

"Tomorrow, we'll be celebrating with sweets!" he said with a laugh. "This table is going to be a hit. It's my best work!" He picked up the last of the dirty banana leaves we ate upon, wiped it, and placed it with the rest in a corner. We would hopefully be using them again tomorrow if my father's sale went well.

"My dear, it is. I know it," my mother replied. My father kissed her on the cheek. I looked at them together. My father's bulky arms—arms you could only get if you spent your days hacking away at wood—were wrapped around my mother's body. He made her look like a tiny, fragile china doll.

"Papa, can I come? I want to see the market!" my sister piped in. I sighed. Zaffirah asked this every day, knowing the answer.

"No, Zaffirah. You know it's too dangerous. There are bad people there," my father said firmly. He picked her up and put her on his back, barely struggling. Almost ten, she was getting too big for that now. "I don't want anyone touching my beautiful little girl."

Zaffirah's lips turned down in frown. "It's not fair," she moaned. "I want to see the outside, like you and Mumma!"

Zaffirah and I were not allowed past our slum walls. Every time we asked to leave, we were met with warnings of the dangers of the outside world. I now knew it was useless to ask, but Zaffirah had yet to learn.

"Shhh, how about you help me set up the donkey cart?" he said, trying to pacify her. "And then, you come back here, okay?"

It worked. She nodded, and my father put her down. He took her small hand in his as he left. "Bye bye, Mumma," she called without a second glance back.

My father would let her feed the donkey a bite of rotten carrot, and she would laugh as his coarse hairs tickled her hand. I had never seen anyone take so much pleasure in feeding an animal as my sister did.

I looked at my mother as she rubbed her dark-ringed eyes and sat down on the pillow beside the crate. She had spent most of the day and the previous nights sewing clothes to sell. Colored threads were strewn on the floor by the sewing machine. She was trying to complete the sequin-shaped tiara on one of her white shirts. The little girls would love it. Playing pretend princess, how could they not love it? Sometimes, my father's furniture didn't bring in enough for us to eat, and my mother would try to help. Recently, we had been having one of those times.

"Isra, go take the baskets to the river. I'll catch up with you in a while."

"No, the only thing you should be catching up on is sleep," I insisted. "I can wash the clothes."

She sighed, and I could tell that she was too tired to put up the fight she usually would on this topic. I picked up the baskets of clothes and left her, hoping she would truly try to rest rather than take up her sewing again.

I had barely taken a few steps out of the door before Farid appeared, smiling.

"Need some help?" he asked, shaking his head like a small puppy dog. Sweat dripped down his forehead and past his cheek. He held a misshapen football in his hands. I would never understand why boys liked that silly game so much.

Sweaty and disgusting as he was, I was glad to see him. These baskets were heavy. "How do you feel about holding both?" I teased.

"Well, you and I both know my Superman strength is unquestionable, but do I really *want* to hold both?"

I tilted my head, pursed my lips, and opened my eyes wide. "Please?"

He snorted and took the baskets from me. His precious, dirty ball, he pushed into my chest.

A drop of water fell on my back and trickled down my spine. My hand automatically went to the wet space on my skin. More drops fell like tiny, cold pinpricks.

"Come on!" I yelled at Farid as I started to run. "The clothes will get wet!"

He feigned confusion and stood where he was as I ran under the shade of a tree. "Please, do enlighten me, how do you wash these clothes without them getting wet?"

"I have magic hands," I shouted over the rain.

"Oh yes. How could I forget?"

I shrugged. I could see that water had begun to collect in the clothes-basket Farid was holding. He walked slowly toward me, grinning. Before I could even think about moving, he had splashed me with rainwater and taken off in a sprint in the other direction, the clothes forgotten on the ground. I screamed in shock and threw the ball at him. It missed him, of course—by a landslide. Forgetting myself, I chased him around the tree where he had dumped our clothes. He ran past the well, and I followed. He was so much faster than me. I had to stop. My breath came heavy from my chest as I heard his friendly laughter from behind and then, ever so softly, an apology. The anger melted off my body. I sighed and laughed with him, the rain dripping down our faces.

When the rain finally subsided to a drizzle, we collected the clothes, which were now much dirtier than they were before, and walked together to the river. I hated washing clothes alone, and having Farid to talk to was always nice. Well, *always* was overstating it, but if I was being completely honest, most of the time I did enjoy his company.

I watched the spiders dance between the mud islands on the surface of the greenish water before I dropped the clothes into the river. Other women had crowded around too. This was the only place we could wash our clothes. Farid's eyes sank to the ground, and he bent his head. I nudged his shoulder. I followed his gaze as he looked up at the other people around the river.

The women were staring directly at us. A plump, hook-nosed woman turned to the short woman beside her and whispered in her ear. Her eyes were cold, and she had scrunched up her huge nose in an expression of disgust. Why was she looking at us like that?

Farid cleared his throat. "I should go," he mumbled. I almost stopped him, but just at that moment, I realized I knew why we were getting those looks. I was here alone with Farid. Sometimes, I forgot that Farid was a boy, and I was not allowed to be alone with him. It was a stupid rule, but I nodded nonetheless.

Farid left as silently as he had appeared, and I washed the clothes alone, without saying a word to anyone. I came home to find my mother asleep. Zaffirah was in her corner too, snoring softly. My father would be returning at any moment. I couldn't sleep till he did. It had become a habit, waiting to hear his heavy breath as he walked through the door from a hard day's work. I picked up my mother's white shirt, threaded a needle and attempted to sew the remaining sequins to finish the tiara.

I didn't sleep that night. Or the nights that came after.

Three

Farid

I hardly knew him. Isra told me they never found a body, but after a week of waiting and a disheartening news article, I guess they had decided it was time to accept the inevitable. You would never be able to tell that anyone hated him. So many people died in our slum from starvation, sickness, and God knew what else, but he was one of the few for whom a funeral was held. At that time, I almost aspired to be like him. I didn't want to be forgotten like everyone else when I died.

Families from all over the slum flocked to his service. There were older couples with their shoulders sagging under the familiar weight of death's complacent visit, and younger ones with their eyelids swollen with sorrow.

I saw a little girl tug at Isra's hand. She was in a dress that I imagined was once white, but was now a dirty, ashen color. Her eyes were tearless. "Is Mikal Uncle really gone?" she asked. Her thumbs twined together to form the shape of a butterfly. She beat her palms and lifted her hands toward the sky to emphasize her point. I wondered what he had meant to her.

My father was here too. His jaw moved side to side as he chewed on his *paan*. When he opened his mouth to speak, I saw glimpses of the scarlet color that stained his teeth. I hated him for that habit. That, and his fondness for alcohol. Money that could have been well spent was wasted on him. He was telling someone the story I had heard so often, about how Mikal had helped build our house. He was telling it with a big, red smile.

"Everything we needed, he gave us! Can you believe it? Everything, I tell you!" He moved his hands in big gestures to emphasize how much *everything* was. "Never had a leaky roof, my house has!" That wasn't a lie. Our house was one of the few with no holes in our tin roof.

If it were not for my mother and her harsh words, I would have been certain that Mikal had made no enemies in his lifetime, only friends too late in returning his kindness. Now, weighted with guilt, they were at his funeral, hoping to do the only thing they could: offer prayers.

One man played sheikh. He read a verse from the Quran, and the others echoed his leading *Du'a*. They prayed that Mikal would have an uncomplicated journey from the world of the living to the world of the dead. They prayed that the unkind deeds he had committed would be forgiven. They prayed that he would achieve entry to heaven. Their voices reverberated, an apology said too late.

Isra was not crying like I'd expected her to be. I knew she was fond of her father. She was fond of her whole family. They got along much better than mine, from what I had heard her tell me. She was staring at the ground, expressionless. I hoped that I would have a moment alone to talk to her. She had been keeping her distance. Our conversations were shorter, and she had often been making excuses to get away from me. I knew they were excuses because her hands would get sweaty, and she would wipe them over and over again on her clothes. She was stupid to think she could lie to me, of all people.

I raised my hand to wave at her when she finally looked up, but her gaze went straight through me. I turned to see what she was looking at. For a second, I almost thought I saw a statue of a cat on two feet. It was so far away, I couldn't be sure. I squinted, and it was gone.

We came home later that night, after the funeral. My mother was furious. I had never seen her so angry in my life.

"How could you?" she hissed. Her green eyes were cold stones, standing out in her creased face. "He was a disgusting man. He didn't deserve your prayers," she said, raising her voice so it was barely softer than a yell.

My father walked toward her and held her wrists. "Shhh," he murmured.

"You told me you wouldn't go," she whimpered. "You promised you wouldn't go!" she cried, clenching her hands into fists and narrowing her eyes. She was trying desperately to control her fury, but to no avail.

My brother entered the room. "What's wrong?" he asked. He almost sounded like, for once in his useless life, he cared.

"Nothing, Asad," my father said quickly.

My mother glanced at him and the corners of her lips turned up in a cruel grin. "You're a fool," she spat in my father's face, before pushing him away as roughly as she could. He staggered back, barely able to keep himself from falling to the ground. He had a body made out of sticks, tied together with flimsy strings. I was surprised a gust of wind hadn't blown him away from our lives already.

"You're all fools!" my mother screamed.

My father simply ignored her and nestled into a chair with a bottle of whiskey. He kissed the glass lips of the bottle with a tenderness that he had never been able to show his wife.

Asad followed in suit of my mother and pushed past me, but just before he left, he whispered in my ear. "This is your fault. You and your stupid girlfriend and her damn father!"

I grabbed him by the cuff of his shirt, glad that, despite him being older, I was taller than him. He flinched back, holding up his hands.

"Don't come near me again," I snarled, then let him go. He backed away like a dog that had just been whipped. I couldn't help but smile.

Four

Isra

"Zaffirah, behind you!" I shrieked at my sister. She ducked just in time. My mother grabbed the nearest thing to her—a wooden chair this time. She flung it at the area where Zaffirah had stood just seconds ago. The flimsy chair crashed with a thud onto the table, breaking into three separate pieces. One leg here. One leg there. And the body somewhere else altogether.

My mother's head fell back as she let out a string of harsh cackles. Her whole body convulsed as her hysterics overpowered her. Her eyebrows had lowered and were drawn together above her icy gaze. My sister glared back at her. I could feel the electric current, generated from their anger, pulsing through the air between them.

My gaze followed Zaffirah as she leapt out from under the table and started running, my mother close behind her. She caught up to Zaffirah, grabbed her arm, spun her around, and then slapped her. I winced. The noise ricocheted off the corners of our house. The smack was like the crack of a whip.

Zaffirah stood motionless, staring at the woman before her. Her left cheek was crimson, and her eyes had filled with tiny crystal tears. I ran to my sister's defense, and with the soft pad of my thumb, I gently brushed away the falling jewels. Turning away from Zaffirah, I watched the woman, bitter thoughts seething in my mind. It was a daily routine now: the beatings, the slaps, the splintered furniture, the blue bruises. That woman was not our mother.

Three weeks had passed since my father's death, and two weeks since my father's funeral. My mother had suffered the worst, though she had always been careful never to allow her face to betray any emotion. She tried to hold back sobs, turning them into tearless coughs. Like a parasite, sorrow ate at her from the inside, and she allowed it. With each day that went by her sadness increased, multiplied even, but still she wouldn't let it out. Just as a balloon too full of air eventually bursts, a person too full of sadness eventually breaks. Fractures like a cracked bone. Shatters like glass. Snaps like a rubber band.

Everything was different now. My mother, insane, and my sister, so easily angered. They fought so often that I knew in my head what would happen next. If you could call it fighting. They were characters, part of a monotonous script—almost halfway through now. Zaffirah said her line, and my mother did her part. She had no lines. Her insanity had driven her almost speechless. Someone else was now running the mechanics of her body, and she didn't stand a chance against him.

"Stop!" I yelled. "Leave her alone."

My mother grinned. It was a strange smile that didn't match the unhappiness in her eyes. She picked up another chair and threw it. I jumped to the side just in time, but otherwise, reacted little. The woman, exhausted from ruining the furniture we had managed to put together just yesterday, and the day before, turned and slid through the curtain splitting our room. I was glad. I could hardly bear to see the monster that wore my mother's face.

"Isra, I don't want do this anymore. I can't . . ." Zaffirah said softly.

"I know," I whispered.

Crrrrr-Eeeekkk. We turned simultaneously as the curtain-door to my mother's room slipped open. The doorway remained empty. "Zaff, do you smell that?"

"It smells like burnt *chapatti* . . . . Is she . . . is she burning something?" A vision flashed in my head, of the house burning helplessly, a silhouette of orange and red flames. I shook the thought away.

"Listen . . ." I murmured. We stepped closer. She was whispering something.

"*Deala Roma Fae.*"

Her whispers echoed around me, drawing me toward her. "*Ddddeaaalllaaa Rrrrroooommmaaa Ffffaaaaeeee.*" As I came nearer, her voice softened. The words were now barely audible, but they maintained their strange power over me.

"Isra." Zaffirah yanked at my arm, snapping my trance. I jerked to face her, a sinking feeling inside me. My heart felt as though it was drowning in a pool of its own blood.

"We have to stop her," I murmured.

Zaffirah shook her head vigorously. "I'm not going in there."

"Okay, stay here. I have to see what she's doing." I didn't wait for Zaffirah's response. I pushed open the curtain and went to the woman I called my mother. She turned to me. Her face was chalky, and her pupils so dilated that both her eyes were completely black. She continued chanting. I held back a shudder as I watched her.

Flames licked her fingers, but she showed no pain. I tried to pry the burning object out of her hands, but it was too hot. I could hardly touch her. All I could do was watch helplessly as her skin bubbled with red and white blisters.

"Mumma?" I called softly. "Mumma, please."

She stopped chanting and looked up at me. Her eyes were almost their normal brown again. As soon as she noticed the skin on her hands burning, she threw the object to the ground and fell to her knees. What she'd dropped was an amulet.

The color was a magnificent red, like the color you see when you rub the palms of your hands against your eyes as the morning sun rests upon your eyelids. It was a color that I thought should not have been in the wavelengths of light the human eye could observe. An electric, scarlet red with filaments of black, silver, and gold. I couldn't shift my eyes away from it. Not even to look at my mother.

"Keep it safe. Protect it with your life," she gasped out. "Now, go!" she screamed before the darkness in her eyes came back, and my mother was lost to me again.

Those words were the last sane words I ever heard from my mother. I picked up the no- longer-burning amulet and ran out of the room. Zaffirah was waiting.

I took a breath to steady myself before I grabbed her hand and pulled her out of the house.

Five

Isra

I felt like I had lost a limb, but in truth, I had lost a lot more than that, because people are defined by their relationships. Every single one is a thread in our mind that wraps neatly to make the nest of emotions we live in. Two of those threads—at the very core of my nest—had snapped, and now, I felt nothing. All I wanted was to sleep and forget about everything that happened. It would be only too easy to convince myself that everything I had seen was a dream.

I looked up and met the evening sun's merciless glare. The heat draped itself over me like a prickly coat that was two sizes too small, pinching my shoulders. Angry, red clouds were starting to fill the sky. It would be dark soon, and we would be without the safety of a roof over our heads.

"Come on, we can't stay here. When it gets dark . . . it's not safe. We have to find somewhere to sleep for the night," I breathed.

I held out my hand, and Zaffirah clasped it. Her lips almost parted in a reassuring smile. She had my mother's smile. The smile before she went mad. It was so beautiful, you would forget about everything else just to stop and stare. She had my mother's everything. Her curly, chestnut hair. Her cocoa, almond eyes. Her small, pixie ears. And the small mole below her left eye. The more I tried not to think about it, the more it crossed my mind. She was a copy, and I would never see the original again.

My feet tugged me forward. Somewhere along the way, the loud claps of our feet had turned into a soft dragging. We were getting closer to the main city. Buildings were taking shape on the horizon.

I could see the thin sheen of sweat that covered my sister and plastered dark strands of hair onto her cheeks. Her expression reflected mine. Every cell in my body groaned a symphony of fatigue. The blisters on the soles of my feet were stinging from the salty beads of sweat in my sandals, but I could do nothing to make it hurt any less. We walked in silence, unable to find the energy to speak.

"Look." Zaffirah's voice cracked from disuse. I followed her gaze. She was pointing at a boy with hair that curled down to his ears. It was tinged almost orange with dirt, making it lighter than it really was. I didn't need to be a mind reader to know what Zaffirah was thinking. Lost and helpless, she hoped he would make our worries go away. So did I. It was strange, clinging onto the possibility of help from a stranger. Why would he help us?

We walked closer. His back was turned, and he was sitting on the ground. As soon as we were within earshot, he turned and jumped up with an agile speed that I would never have expected. He looked just barely a year older than me. Towering at around six feet, his body was hard with muscles, but thin, the result of physical work rather than malnourishment. The streets had served him better than many.

"What are you doing here?" he growled in a bearlike voice. A sliver of silvery metal glinted in his left hand—a knife. I grabbed my sister's wrist and felt the muscles in my legs tighten, ready to run at the first sign of a threat. But when I looked at the boy's face, I felt . . . different. His eyes were the color of fertile earth and flecked with spots of honey gold, but it wasn't just the color, it was the expression that they held. He continued to stare at me. As he did, I saw the strangest thing happen in his eyes. The brown and gold swirled around each other—in rings. I blinked, and his eyes instantly went back to normal. I wondered if I had imagined it.

I didn't know what it was about him, but I felt safe. I felt as though he was poised to defend me rather than hurt me, though the knife pointing at me would beg to differ. I looked around at the other children that I seemed to have missed before. They were standing now, backing the boy. From the look of it, the boy was the one that gave the orders around here. One word from him and we could either be worshipped, or killed to be sacrificed to the Devil.

I took in the area. It was deserted. There were no buildings other than a single, abandoned parking lot that stood nearby. A bridge-like structure sheltered most of the area. If you knelt low enough, other people walking by wouldn't see you. That was why I hadn't seen the boy until he was only meters away.

"Hello? Hey! Are you deaf?" The boy waved his knife in my face. I forgot that he was still waiting for an answer. I tried to give him one, but my tongue, heavy in my mouth, remained soundless. Words that I couldn't bring to my lips floated in the air around me. All I could think about was the burning fire in my throat. I had never felt a thirst so intense. I could deal with hunger. There was always a shortage of food in my slum, but water was easily accessible. The well was always full. Sometimes dirt-ridden and contaminated, but always there.

"We've run away from home. Our father is dead, and our mother is . . ." Zaffirah stopped, then took a deep breath. "We've nowhere else to go." My sister answered for me in a wispy voice that was almost softer than a murmur. I wondered if he heard it. We were so tired that suddenly, I couldn't care less. I could sleep right there—on the sandy ground. When your bones were brittle with exhaustion, dirt and grit probably felt like feathers plucked from the world's softest bird. Who needed his permission, anyway?

The boy flicked his wrist. The motion seemed to be intended for the back-up squad behind him. They took a step away from the boy as he turned to face them. We stayed where we were. A girl came forward and handed the boy something without speaking. The two looked as though they were having a conversation that didn't require words. The boy nodded, and the girl disappeared, dissolving back into the crowd of children. Seconds passed before the boy finally turned around, no longer with the knife in hand.

"We are helping you; try not to forget our kindness. You may sleep amongst us tonight. Keep this, it gets cold after sunset." He thrust a mud-stained, sandy blanket into my hands. It felt heavier than I would have imagined a blanket to be. From underneath its layers of dirt and grit, I unwrapped a plastic water bottle and passed it to Zaffirah. I couldn't help the smile that tugged at the corners of my lips. Water and a safe place to sleep. I tried to thank the boy, but he saved me the trouble, quickly walking away.

Zaffirah swallowed the water hungrily as I placed the blanket on the ground. I guided her to it, resisting the temptation to snatch the bottle out of her hand and gulp it down myself. It was going to be a long night. I gazed at the moon casting a hazy glow above me. Having had as much water as her stomach desired, Zaffirah lay down and squirmed for a few minutes before I could finally hear her soft, steady snores. At that moment, the world looked as though it was touched by God's silver hand. With that thought in mind, reality blended into the world of palpable fantasy, and I slept peacefully for the first time in a long time.

I woke the next morning, watching as the dull blue of the sky lit up with the fiery heat of its inhabitant, the sun. The other children I'd seen yesterday had dispersed, along with the boy. My nose instantly pricked at the intense smell of gasoline in the air around me. I could almost feel its heavy heat closing in on me, though I knew that there was no fire here to set it off . . . at least, not yet.

I glanced up and saw food set out on the ground a couple of meters away from where I was sleeping, centered carefully on a filth-covered mat. A mat so dirty that it was almost impossible to tell its color. Not that I cared to find out, because the food was what caught my eye. There were an assortment of fruits and vegetables surrounding a plate filled with pieces of bread and a bowl of buttery curry. My mouth watered at the aromatic smell laced with spices and herbs wafting in the air, almost overpowering the scent of the gasoline.

A strong, physical urge grew within me, encouraging me to have a bite of the soft, supple bread and a taste of the curry. I had never smelled anything so mouth-watering. My stomach groaned and I got up, scrambling over to the setting like I had lost control of my own body. I popped my finger into the orange, creamy curry and lifted it to my mouth.

The savory taste of paprika and onion instantly swathed my tongue, introducing my taste buds to a delicious new flavor.

"Mmmmmm." I'd always thought that my mother was a good cook, but seasoning was only affordable to the wealthy. My mother simply met our basic needs; trying to make the food incredibly appetizing was not high on her priority list.

"Hey you! What do you think you're doing? Get out of here! Stupid girl."

I looked up, my eyes wide as I took in the husky voice of the tall boy who stood above me. I hadn't seen him the night before. He had a crooked nose, which looked as though it had been broken more than once and was now unable to heal. A pink scar ran across the side of his left temple, down to the tip of his ear. But behind his mangled attributes, I could see the similarities in his features to that of the boy I'd seen yesterday.

However, this boy, unlike the one before, appeared more sinister than the last, and he wasn't even carrying a knife. Sensing the danger I was in, I clumsily leapt up, but he was faster than me. Somehow, I knew he would be. His speed was like that of the boy last night—inhuman. Before I knew it, he had me in a headlock. I could smell the damp sweat from his arms as he tightened his grip around my neck.

In that moment, I wished I could materialize away. Turn into a bird and just fly into the sky far, far away. Just for that moment—but, of course, that didn't happen. Life was not a fairy tale. I, of all people, should have known that by now.

"I think she needs a lesson, don't you? Show her what happens to those who steal our food!" another mocking male voice called out from behind me.

The boy didn't need any more provoking. Using his curled fist, he punched me in the middle of my belly. I doubled over as pain, like shards of glass, sliced through my insides. My heart squeezed for a second. He must have hit me more than once. I was stronger than one punch. I wasn't that weak. Was I?

"Kasim, your brother allowed her to sleep amongst us, and this is how she repays his sympathy? It's disgusting," another one snarled.

"He what? Ahh, my brother isn't one to turn away a *poor, lost girl*. I must warn him about taking strangers under his wing," he scoffed. He grabbed me by the collar of my shirt and pulled me to my feet.

"This is for him." He grinned.

Thwack. He kicked my shin. I fell to my knees while my vision blurred behind spots of black and red. I willed them to go away, but there they stayed—unwilling to leave. My head spun around like an out of control merry-go-round. Round and round. Never stopping. Round and round.

You know the game every child has played at least once in his or her life. Where you cross your arms in an *X* and clasp hands with your partner. Then you spin around as fast as you can, watching the world smudge into distortion. Then, you stop and the disorientation hits you like a whirlwind. Everything is moving, jerking left, jolting right. You're in a giant earthquake.

Everything went black. I was blind. I had lost my sight, and yet the pain remained. It flared like an inferno, from my stomach up to my throat. I coughed as copper-tasting blood surged out of my mouth.

"Stop . . . please . . . I'm sorry . . ." I cried between coughs of blood. I tried to use my eyes, but still, I couldn't see a thing. I could feel myself slipping away. I was feeling more and more dizzy—light-headed—and then, the pain was gone.

Just like that. I could no longer feel my body. My soul plunged into eternal darkness. I was in oblivion. My whole body was numb. I wondered, for a second, if this was what death felt like. But I couldn't be dead. Not yet. I had to stay alive for Zaffirah. I ignored the tempting call of death, with its promise of relief. I wouldn't let it take me. I forced myself to feel. I had to bring the pain back. I needed to be alive. I wasn't ready to die.

"Kasim, you didn't have to hurt her, you know. She would have moved . . ." a familiar voice said. His speech wasn't layered with sarcasm. The owner of the voice lifted my lifeless body while I hovered blindly above it, trying to regain control. I couldn't help but notice that the boy had the sweetest smell of fresh-cut grass and clean sweat.

"What do you care, brother? Who are you? Her guardian angel? Oh, wait . . ." I heard the same terrifying, husky voice taunt. I waited for an answer, but I heard nothing. The boy had nothing more to say on the matter. He put my body down softly, and I listened as his companion's footsteps slapped the ground further and further away, until there was nothing but me, my body, and the boy.

Then, just like that, the pain was back . . . but it was a different kind of pain . . . a burning. I felt it under my skin. Prickling like tiny, red-hot needles. I could feel my body again. First my feet, then my hands, and then the rest of me. I opened my eyes to see another set of brown eyes staring at me, but I knew they were neither mine nor my sister's. *My sister*! I trembled and tried to get myself up, only to fall back down again; he caught me, just before I hit the ground. His arms held me for less than a second before lightly putting me down. That millisecond was enough for me to feel the charged sparks his fingertips emitted. They were feverishly hot, almost burning my skin.

"Just relax for a minute, will you?" he snapped. It was the same boy I had seen yesterday, the one who had given Zaffirah and me the water. The boy whose features I could see in the one that hurt me.

"What are you doing?" I mumbled, when I had finally gained enough energy to open my mouth.

I looked around, taking in where I was for the first time. It looked like some sort of shelter. The walls were a dark grey, made of discolored cement. The ground here was not dirty like it had been where I slept last night. Instead, it was dusty.

"What's it look like I'm doing?" he retorted. "Here, drink. It will ease the pain," he grumbled, nestling into a corner of the shelter.

I stared at him as he passed me a plastic cup half-filled with a thick, amber liquid. I sniffed it, and the metallic scent tickled the insides of my nose. "Why should I trust you?" I asked, carefully pushing the cup away from me. I didn't want his pity or his help. I didn't need him.

He sighed. "Whatever I would have wanted to do to you, I would have done already. Believe me. I'd love to see you fight me off while you're writhing in pain on the floor."

He pushed the cup back. I stared at it, and then gently traced the rim.

"Why are there no children in here?" I asked.

He watched the pattern my fingers were making as I played with the cup. He knew I didn't want to drink it. His eyes narrowed. "There used to be cars here, but something happened. A fire. The kids think it's haunted." He shrugged. "Now quit stalling and *drink,* or the pain won't be leaving anytime soon."

I paused for a few seconds. Seeing my hesitation, he finally came closer and took the cup from my hands. He sipped it and then gently held it to my lips. Deciding to trust him, I drank it. It left the bitter aftertaste of iron.

I hadn't really noticed the pain before, but as soon as he mentioned it, it was back. An excruciating throbbing all over my body that was impossible to ignore. "Ahhh!" I gasped.

He was at my side within seconds. "Are you okay? Where does it hurt?" He did a good job of looking worried. I couldn't tell for certain if his emotions were genuine or not.

I placed the palm of my hand on the leg that had been kicked. As the boy lowered his hands to inspect my leg, I almost jerked away from his touch, but I forced myself to stay still as a statue. The boy worked his fingers slowly, massaging my leg, relieving me of the pain. The blistering current in his fingers was ever-present.

I glanced at the boy's angular face. His dark lashes were lowered over his eyes, and he was chewing his lower lip in concentration. He noticed me staring, and I quickly looked away.

"I know he was your brother. Who are you?" I probed.

"The resemblance is hard to ignore, isn't it? Even with his screwed up face. They call me Ammun." His gaze fell to his hands. He pulled them away from my leg and began fiddling with a thin, white bracelet tied around his wrist. Underneath the bracelet, I could see the remnants of dirt, a dirty golden color.

I shook my head, trying think clearly again, and then it all came back in a sudden rush. Something I was forgetting. Something I promised I would protect. I tried standing, but ended up almost collapsing to the floor . . . again. He caught me. Just like before. Softly lowering me to the ground.

"I need to get out of here!" I said.

"Calm down. Breathe. Now, tell me what's wrong?" Ammun asked, looking directly at me for the first time. This time, I was certain his concern was real.

"My sister . . . *where is my sister?*" I screeched at him. I didn't give him time to answer, though to his credit, he looked as though he meant to. "He took her, didn't he?" I screamed. He looked at me, his face expressionless.

My fingers clenched and blood pounded through my head. I was supposed to protect her.

He knelt beside me and sighed. "I'll take you to her. Just stop *crying*, dammit." He jostled my shoulders, forcing me to meet his glare. He was right. Sitting here weeping like a spineless insect was wasting time. I wiped my tears with the hem of my sleeve and swallowed the lump in my throat.

"Now," I growled, hoping that my voice came out as menacingly as I had intended.

"Put away the claws," he replied without a smile and started walking, barely waiting for me to catch up.

I urged my feet to stand—to once again hold my weight, but I wobbled awkwardly, like a toddler learning how to walk for the first time. Before I fell for the third time, he placed his hands around my waist, ever so lightly, supporting my weight until I could finally stand. I leaned on his arm as we walked, eventually ending up back at the same place I remembered spending the night in.

He stopped a couple of meters away from Zaffirah and turned his head, gesturing for me to follow his gaze. She was exactly where I had left her, buried in the muddy blanket, still sound asleep. Her dark brown hair fanned out beneath her head in a halo. Her cherub-like face had the slight trace of a smile across her lips. I couldn't bring myself to interrupt the serenity of her sleep.

The sun was fully up now, shining bright. Zaffirah should be getting up soon enough. A sun that bright couldn't keep anyone sleeping for long. I glanced at Zaffirah from my peripheral vision; I was right. Sure enough, she rubbed the sleep out of her eyes and I watched her open them. Her heavy lids lifted to reveal her big, brown doe eyes.

"Good morning, Isra—*urghhh*—what's that smell?" She smiled and yawned. Her lips parted, giving way to the curved, white section of her teeth. I smiled back.

"The smell is gasoline," Ammun explained. "It keeps people away because of its—uh—*flammable* qualities. This place is close to a gas station with a leak. I don't know why you didn't smell it last night. I mean, can you really ignore this?" He gestured to the air around him.

I took a huge sniff of the air and then broke into a fit of coughing.

The smell was for protection, I realized. Murderers, kidnappers, and thieves wouldn't risk their lives coming here. On the off chance that someone lit a flame, the whole area would go up in smoke.

"If you don't pay attention to the details, you'll be dead in seconds," he said quietly.

"It's ironic how my lack of attention brought me here to safety," I scoffed.

He took a step toward me. "Think, what if I hadn't helped you? What if I had pierced my knife straight through your heart?" he replied, his finger jabbing softly into my chest. The tips of them were sparking again. I felt the heated electricity run races over my skin. "Honestly, we don't need more people sharing this already overcrowded space. Take a look around."

I shrugged, half hoping that the knife he carried had never touched human flesh, but I knew the probability of that was fairly low.

"Well, then I guess we owe you a thank you, Ammun . . . for not killing us," I muttered.

He ignored my comment. "Come on—" He paused. I waited for him to continue. "I'll buy you some breakfast; it will be left-over food from the stalls, whatever they have. You'll learn not to be picky when you're on the streets."

You learn not to be picky when you're poor and living in a slum too, I thought to myself, but said nothing.

Hours later, we were sitting on the ground eating *chapattis,* just like my mother used to make. So much for *stale* food. The *chapattis* were warm and delicious. That was all Ammun could afford, which was, to be fair, a lot more than I could. I sank my teeth into the nutty flavor of the bread, letting it tickle my taste buds. It was velvety soft, like a damp, light brown blanket. My last meal was almost two days ago, and I was starving.

"Thank you for the food," Zaffirah said graciously. He nodded in return, expressionless. The gratitude Zaffirah had offered had almost no effect on him.

"It was a one-time thing, so don't get used to it. Use those big, brown eyes until you find a real job. You can beg for money on the streets in the downtown area. Begging's easy. You won't get much money, but it's better than nothing."

He was right. There were days when we had fed on nothing in my family. As rare as my father tried to make those days, once in a while it was inevitable. Even poverty had a price. I licked my fingers clean and got up. "I guess we should be going then."

He nodded. But just as we were walking away, Ammun called out to us. "Wait! Take this." The same knife that he had threatened to kill me with was in his hand. This time, the hilt was toward us—a peace offering.

"What about you?" I asked.

"What? You think I keep only one knife? Believe me, I'm a walking arsenal of deadly devices." I looked to see the spark of humor in his face, but there was none. He wasn't joking. "Here, take it. Better safe than sorry." He pushed the knife toward me.

I glanced at the elegant arc of lustrous metal fixed into the dark, solid-carved hilt. It was a beautiful knife. He wrapped a white cloth around the sharp-edged silver and placed the knife in my open palms. My eyes met his, and I smiled at him gratefully, already feeling safer with the knife in my possession.

"Be careful, okay? I didn't waste my time helping you and giving you food, only to see you . . ." He didn't finish, but I understood what he meant. I nodded an okay. He turned away, but almost instantly turned back around to face me again, as if he was forgetting something.

"Sometimes, I polish shoes in the downtown area. Wait for me by the shoe shop around the corner. It's next to a Chinese restaurant. You can't miss it. Maybe we can walk back together."

He smiled at me. I was surprised. It was the first time I had seen him smile. It lit up his whole face. Though he had never seemed like the angry, violent sort that his brother was, he'd still appeared . . . unapproachable. Yes, that was the only word to describe him. But when he smiled, that unapproachability disappeared and he discharged nothing but comforting warmth. I had to physically pull myself away from that smile.

Six

Isra

A bare-footed girl stood a few meters in front of me with her right arm outstretched. Her lips moved, but no sound escaped them. Her left hand rested upon the head of a golden dog, barely two feet tall. It was hiding behind the girl, peeking at the people walking past.

Beside them, an old hunched woman dragged a cart full of her wares, stopping in front of possible buyers. Two girls, weighed down in silver chains and golden bracelets, flagged her down. They picked up her little trinkets, twirling them between their painted fingers. The bigger of the two forced one of the woman's bracelets, sizes too small, onto her wrist. It snapped immediately and the girl put its broken pieces back on the woman's cart. The other one grabbed a handful of earrings. A few fell from her clumsy hands onto the ground. When the girl made no attempt to return the things to the cart, the woman bent over to pick up her precious goods, her face twisted in agony as she rested a hand on her hip. Snatching the remainder of the jewelry still in the girls' hands, the woman demanded payment for their carelessness. The girls stubbornly shook their heads and walked away to another seller, who bowed repeatedly to them, only too eager to please his new customers.

The idea of begging had never been as unappealing to me as it was now. I hated looking small and vulnerable for the affluents to pity me. I didn't want them to consider me a charity case . . . but I needed their money. I *was* a charity case.

"Isra, look." Zaffirah pointed. She was looking at the little girl I had seen earlier. Mimicking her motion, Zaffirah extended her arm.

"Watch me!" Zaffirah called. She feigned a limp and hobbled to a man with a tie wrapped around the collar of his shirt—so tight that it looked as though it was threatening to choke him in its viper grip. She pulled the sleeve of his shirt, and with a look of sympathy in his eyes, he dropped a few coins in her hand. Zaffirah limped back, grinning. She held up the coins like a trophy she had *earned* and not just conned from a man that was too kind before my very eyes.

"Why were you limping?" I asked.

"I saw that girl do it. I think because she's hurt, she gets more money. I bet she's faking."

I found myself looking at the same little girl with her dog. Underneath her patchwork, torn skirt, her left leg was grotesquely small and curled. Her toes pointed inward.

"Zaff, she really is hurt," I blurted. I turned to see Zaffirah already fake-limping away to her next naïve victim. Blinded by silver, she hadn't heard a word I said.

I couldn't take my eyes off the girl. A dark-haired boy walked toward her. The girl's eyes brightened, and she gave him a big, toothy grin. In return, the boy picked her up and spun her around, finally placing her on his shoulders. I watched the exchange, curiously, from a distance. The little pup almost looked as though he wore a smile too. His tongue hung from his mouth as he panted, and his crooked tail wagged in an eager show of affection.

"I have something for you," the boy declared after he put the girl down. I recognized the sound of his voice and a moment later, I realized that I knew who he was.

"Really?" she asked softly. It was the first time I had heard her speak. Her voice was like a stream in the middle of a deserted land—alone and small.

The boy nodded. "Two things actually," he ventured.

The girl was now having trouble holding back her excitement. She bounced slightly on the spot. "What are they?" she questioned. "Can I see them? Please?"

"Of course you can. They're for you, after all." He laughed and fondly ruffled the girl's dark mass of hair. The girl frowned a little, but the smile was back when the boy's hand went into the pocket of his trousers. As his hand came out again, I saw that his fingers were wrapped around a bottle of apple juice.

"Now, this is the sweetest nectar from the brightest yellow sunflowers that only grow on the moon," he confided. His voice held traces of friendly playfulness. The girl reached out for it and grabbed it from his hands. She shook it back and forth between her palms so the top frothed with yellow bubbles.

"Ooo, would you like to share it with me?" she offered.

He shook his head. "No, it's okay. I have many more bottles at home, don't you worry." His voice wavered slightly. He was lying.

The boy didn't have the arrogant air that surrounded nearly every child born into riches. He wasn't an affluent. He had on a faded t-shirt, ripped at the corner of his shoulder blade, revealing a sliver of his tanned skin. I waited for him to turn around.

"Now come. I have to show you my second present. This one isn't coming to you, you have to go to it." He winked.

I didn't think it was possible, but the girl's smile grew wider as she laced her hand in his and the two of them turned together in my direction.

In Farid's hand was a can of black polish, a rag hung over his shoulders. He was the last person that I wanted to see. He was a reminder of what I had left behind in my slum—a reminder of my mother. I looked away, pretending I hadn't noticed, but it was too late of course. He had seen me.

"*Isra*!" he shouted. He let go of the girl's hand and ran toward me, stopping a few centimeters away. He hesitated, unsure of *how* exactly to greet me, and then decided a hug would be best. If anyone from our slum would have seen us, they would have been shocked at the blatant display of affection. I hugged him back, realizing that, despite everything, I had missed him. He grinned wide before stepping away from me. "I'm glad to see you," he murmured. I couldn't help smiling at that.

The girl darted toward us and was suddenly at his side again, the little pup trailing beside her. She tugged at Farid's shirt, her eyes pleading, and he looked down at her. She was used to having Farid's complete attention, I realized. Having me here meant that Farid did not have eyes only for her.

"Yes, yes, your present, come on." He laughed and met my gaze. "Would you like to come with us?" he asked. "It won't take long, and we're not going far."

"I . . . I don't—"

"Oh, come on now. You're not going to make much money standing here doing nothing, anyway."

I hesitated, looking around for Zaffirah. When I finally spotted her, she seemed lost in her own world.

"Please?" Farid implored.

The little girl was becoming impatient now. The distrust was clear in her eyes. She didn't want me around. That should have been reason enough for me to shake my head and leave, but the truth was I wanted to stay with Farid a little longer.

"Okay," I mumbled, sparing one last glance at Zaffirah. I hated to admit it, but she was doing a good job. Better than I would have done. She was a born actor, and in that moment, she looked so absorbed by her character that I knew it would be a long time before she noticed I was missing. Still, I went to her to let her know I'd be gone.

"I'll be back in a few minutes. Don't go anywhere, okay?" I said, touching her elbow.

"Mhmm." She waved me off distractedly and walked away without a second glance.

Farid led me past the shops. The girl stuck to him like glue. I hadn't seen this brotherly side of Farid before. If I hadn't known any better, I would have thought the two were related by blood, but Farid didn't treat his brothers the way he treated this girl. "This way," he guided.

A large pawnshop stood before us. In the window was a child mannequin wearing a baby blue dress matched with closed, strappy shoes. The clasps were glittering moons, and several small stars had been stitched into the corner of each shoe. The girl pressed her nose to the window. Her eyes were wide with wonder.

Farid laughed as he gently pushed the girl into the shop. He exchanged a few words with the shopkeeper and the shoes were brought out. The girl reached over to stroke them.

"They're beautiful," she whispered.

"Of course they are. They're made from dragon wings and the breath of butterflies." He grinned.

"Truly?" she gasped.

He nodded. "Do you want me to help you try them on?"

The smile never left his face as he bent down and picked up the shoes. The girl sat down and allowed Farid to fit her right leg into the shoe. It was a perfect fit. The girl then lifted her dress and her left foot came into view, bent in an unnaturally odd angle. The little girl's face fell as she realized the dilemma. Farid had forgotten about her leg. I walked over to the girl with an idea playing in my head. I ripped a piece of fabric from my *dupatta* and bent down at the girl's feet. Her eyes were glittering now with tears.

"May I?" I asked. When the girl didn't answer, Farid nodded for her.

"It's okay, Maya," he comforted. *Maya.* So that was her name. I touched her callused and dirty foot. She flinched.

"Does it hurt?" I asked.

"Sometimes," she admitted.

"Maya, close your eyes," Farid suggested. Obediently, her lids fell. "Do you remember the time we picked flowers in Old Ruzzier's garden?" She nodded. "Do you remember the red roses? And the white chambeli? I climbed her tree, and then she chased us out. But we still had her mangoes!" She laughed, nodding at the memory.

Farid indicated that it was okay for me to touch her leg. I got to work. Wrapping the fabric around her leg, I stretched out her toes and covered her foot up to her ankle. She didn't flinch once, too lost in thought to notice. Farid picked up the shoe and passed it to me. I loosened the clasp and lightly coaxed her foot into it.

"All done. Open your eyes," I said. Her eyelashes fluttered. She caught sight of the shoe and grinned.

"Thank you," she breathed, still recovering from the shock of seeing herself in proper shoes.

Farid put an arm around her, half carrying, half lifting her. Maya walked slowly as she got used to the feel of her shoes. Her left leg dragged behind her.

"Thank you, Farid *bhai*," she murmured. She called him brother, and now, I felt he deserved the label of not just respect, but kinship. I had never seen him treat anyone with such kindness.

Farid wrapped Maya in a hug. "I'm glad you like them," he murmured into her hair.

He paid for the shoes. I couldn't tell how much they were, but judging by the worried, concentrated look on his face as the bills left his hand, I knew that they hadn't come cheap. I walked in step with Farid. Maya was a little way ahead, playing with her puppy and dancing in circles in her new shoes.

"Farid, where did you get the money from . . . to pay for her shoes? How did you afford it?"

He cocked his head to one side, as if deciding whether to answer my question or not. "It was easier than you think . . . to get the money. Come, I want to show you something," he said finally. He pulled my wrist and whispered words I couldn't catch into Maya's ear.

"Wait here. Watch us, okay?" he said out loud to me.

I nodded. Maya walked over to a woman in a long, burgundy skirt. She pulled her arm with a tearful look in her eyes, murmured something and pointed at her dog that now lay on the ground whining. The woman walked over to the dog and rubbed the space on his head between his ears. Behind her, I saw Farid's spidery fingers reach into her dark purse. The woman hadn't noticed. Farid pulled out a number of things.

Amongst them was a packet of cigarettes, a wallet, and keys dangling from a studded keychain. He opened the wallet, pulled out a few bills, and then quickly returned the objects to their rightful place. Farid brought his thumbs up, and the moment Maya noticed the gesture, she shook her dog and he rose. The woman got up and, smiling, she walked away clueless to what had transpired behind her back.

"It's easy money," Farid told me as he approached.

"It's wrong."

"I think it's fair. I come here every day, and they give me so little for what I do. I hate polishing shoes." He nudged the rag on his shoulder. "It's demeaning. Their kids have it so easy. They don't even have to work for the money," he complained.

"Farid, that doesn't make stealing okay."

"Oh, don't be such a saint. I don't steal for myself. I'm all Maya has. And my family—we hardly have half a meal a day! Why do we starve while they stuff themselves stupid? I take such little money, I bet they don't even know it's gone!"

I didn't say anything. I didn't know what to say to that. He gave a convincing argument, and I would be lying if I said that I hadn't thought the same thing myself for a long time. Why were some born filthy rich, and others so incredibly poor?

"I can teach you how to do it so they don't notice," he offered.

I shook my head. "No." *Not yet, anyway.*

"Well, it's your loss. You know, I meant what I said before. I'm glad to see you. Everyone thought that you, your sister, and your mother—Kahleen Auntie—were dead . . . . I'm so glad you're okay. But I knew you would be, you're too stubborn to let death take you so easily," he blurted with an easy smile.

I winced as he articulated my mother's name. "Why would they think we're dead?" I asked.

"Don't you know?"

"No. I wouldn't be asking if I did."

"I—I don't—I could be—wrong," he stuttered.

"Wrong about what? For God's sake, Farid, tell me what happened!" He stared at me, his mouth pursed in a tight, thin line. "Please," I begged.

"Your house . . . it went up in flames. Everyone in our slum tried to put the fire out, but they were too late. They could only stop it from spreading. It would've killed a lot of people. Where were you when that was happening? I think if you were at home, you could've stopped it earlier—before it got out of control—" He stopped himself. "I'm sorry."

I felt his unintended accusations hit me like slaps. I blamed myself too . . . for ignoring the vision of my house burning, and for listening to my mother and leaving her to die. But what if she hadn't? What if she was okay? I had to ask. "What happened to my mother?"

"When my father pulled her out of the ruins of your home, they were both badly burned, and they were speaking words no one could understand."

I felt a sigh of relief work its way up to my mouth. She was still alive then! "How is my mother?"

I realized the thread in my mind that I thought had snapped

was still there. The thread that was my relationship with my mother. It was on the verge of breaking, but it hadn't yet.

Farid opened his mouth and then closed it again. There was something he wasn't saying. I waited until he was ready to speak. "Isra, I'm sorry—we tried to help her . . ."

I froze. My vision blurred. The ground moved. I was seeing double. A sharp pang of pain attacked my forehead. I clutched it, trying to remove the agonizing throb. It was useless. The colors from my sight drained away. Everything went black and white, grainy like an old picture. My head pounded to the beat of my heart. This was the moment that the thread truly snapped.

"Isra, are you okay?"

Ba boom. Ba boom. Ba boom.

"Isra?"

Ba boom. Ba boom. Ba boom.

"Isra! Who was that?" Zaffirah snapped her fingers in my face.

The pain finally abandoned my head, leaving behind a mild case of disorientation. Behind Zaffirah, I saw Farid staring at me. I hadn't noticed him move away. It seemed that neither had Zaffirah.

"No one," I murmured, turning away from Farid's gaze.

"But, I saw you talking to someone?"

I shook my head, refusing to say any more. Zaffirah would be better off not knowing.

Seven

Isra

The sun slowly crept away, and the moon took its place. The soft breeze stroked my face gently and played with my hair. It reminded me of my mother, comforting in a way, but torturous nonetheless. A bittersweet memory.

We waited for Ammun. I was so sure that he would come, but he didn't. As the area emptied of life, my sister finally turned toward me.

"Isra, I'm tired. He won't come. I want to go home," she said, echoing what I was thinking. I took her hand and began walking hesitantly, once again with nowhere to go and no one to go to. The feeling of abandonment hung heavy on my heart. We walked past dark and narrow alleyways.

"I *wish* we *could* go home," I murmured.

As I walked, I heard hushed voices behind us. They were male. I strained to hear what they were saying, catching bits and pieces.

"Grab the tall one," one of them said. The man's companion murmured inaudibly. His voice rose at the end of his sentence. It was a question.

"Yeah, I'll take the little one," the other man answered. His voice was the kind that, no matter how hushed he attempted to keep it, you could always hear the words being said as clear as crystal. There was another murmur, and the other man agreed. I turned my eyes to the ground and focused on the vague shadows that were cast by the soft glow of the street lamps. There was my shadow, tall and hazy. Next to it was Zaffirah's. The same, only a little smaller. But that was not all I saw.

I was hoping desperately that my suspicions were mistaken, but they weren't. A shadow lurked behind me. I could make out a second one, blending with Zaffirah's. They were too close. Something was wrong. I felt the tension before I understood why it was there in the first place.

Then, I realized who they were. Snatchers. Kidnappers. They took children. Orphans usually. No one missed us. They would disfigure us. Make us look more pitiful than we already were and force us to beg for money that they later took for themselves. They did other things too. Worse things. My mother had told me terrifying bedtime stories about them as a child.

"If you don't go to sleep, the Snatchers will take you!" she would say.

This is it, I thought. I didn't even have time to panic. I couldn't think. I couldn't run. My feet were stuck, unable to quicken their pace. I pressed my eyes shut with horror as the shadows enclosed us and the strong, beefy hands grabbed us from behind. My mouth opened to let out a scream, but they shoved something into it, asphyxiating my shriek. The arms lifted me effortlessly and threw me into a bag. Submerged in darkness, the rank smell of sweat encased me. I could taste the sour vomit in my mouth. I kicked, lashing out in all directions, but it was no use. The man threw the sack over his shoulder, maliciously laughing as he did so. I was powerless.

My first instinct was to lunge for the bag I had carried around with me ever since we ran away. *The knife*, I thought. *Find the knife. Slit the bag and run.*

Only one problem: The bag on my shoulder was not mine. It was Zaffirah's. I tore it open, frantically searching—simply hoping that I had accidentally decided to put the knife in Zaffirah's bag, but I hadn't. Nothing in there could help me . . . . what was that thrumming? It was unbearably loud and impossible-to-ignore. I rummaged through her bag, eventually finding the source of the noise: the amulet. My fingers brushed across its glowing light. The amulet's clear, vibrating energy pierced my ears.

I grabbed the amulet out of the bag, watching it tremble with power. The red, black, silver, and gold swirled around each other in smoky rings, but I wasn't shocked. I knew exactly what to do with it, like I had known all along, but somehow time had stolen the knowledge from me. In the corner of my head, the cobwebs suddenly brushed away.

I pressed my eyes shut, emptying my mind completely of fear, shoving it away and instead, filling my head with darkness. I imagined myself unconscious, and I felt sight, sound, smell, and touch disappear. Even the force of gravity had no effect on me. I was welcomed back to the oblivion that I had only momentarily visited before.

"Deala Roma Fae." A distant voice flowed from my lips as strange energy uncoiled from deep within me. There was a burst of white lightning, and I opened my eyes. The street had changed to the grey rock walls of a cave, growing more solid as the darkness faded.

I wasn't sure where I was, but I breathed a sigh of relief anyway. This was a safer place to be than the Snatcher's sack. I glanced around, searching for Zaffirah. The hands of panic tightened around my body when I couldn't see her. "Zaff! Zaffirah, where are you?" I called, trying to keep my voice calm and steady. "Zaffirah! Zaffirah!"

And then it came back to me in a sudden rush. There were two sacks. She was not in my sack. There were two men, one behind me and one behind her. They'd had two sacks—one for me, and one for her. They took her. She was gone, and I couldn't help her.

A primal scream escaped my lips, and I continued screaming; for my insane mother, for my dead father, for Ammun, and for my dear, now lost sister. My lungs felt like they were about to erupt, but I couldn't stop. The scream released all of the pain and pressure I had felt since my father died. I curled up into a tight ball, lowered myself to the ground, and cried myself miserably to sleep.

I dreamt of us together again, all of us together as we were, before one tragedy after another tore us apart. We smiled with contentment as we talked about our day, fortunate to have each other; but the happiness didn't last long, even in my dreams. The dream changed. I watched reluctantly as the scene turned cloudy and died away to reveal the distorted parody I was afraid to call my mother. Her hair, in messy tangles, framed her ghost-like face.

"*Deala Roma Fae,*" she whispered. "*Deala Roma Fae.*" Her lips revealed teeth so sharp and white, they were more animal than human. Her whispers filled my head, soft at first, but gradually louder and more urgent.

"*DealaromafaeDealaromafaeDealaromafae.*" My mother's voice was suddenly accompanied by another voice, and then another—more voices joined the terrible chant. The cacophony of sounds hammered in my head. I jerked up, and the parody of my mother disappeared, along with the terrible sound.

My back ached as I tried to sit up. Tiny rocks were embedded into my skin. I brushed them away, exposing the red indentations that they'd left behind. I shook my head, trying to leave the memory of the dream behind. Whispers of a strange, sweet melody crept into my ears, calming my worries. I rubbed the sleep out of my eyes. Above me were tiny spots of light, like stars, but painted with every color present in a rainbow . . . . I had never seen or heard anything like them before.

Hypnotized by their song, I let myself be led to the entrance of the cave. Only when I stepped out did all my memories come back.

I scanned the cold, vast expanse of the night sky, dotted with white specks, embracing the earth in a bitter hug. The half-moon was smiling down, laughing. As though my pain gave it pleasure.

Grey thunderclouds filled the sky and dampness stole into my hair. A cold splatter sliced through the air and onto my skin. A flash of lightning struck out, and the wet dissonance of a thunderstorm began. With each tear of rain that fell to the ground, a new nail was pounded into my head. I pulled myself back inside the cave, but there was no point. My hair was already drenched, along with my only pair of clothes. My arms wrapped around my body in an attempt to stop my teeth chattering from the cold.

I felt the weight of the amulet burn into the palm of my right hand. I opened it to look at the stone. The skin over my palm was red, streaked with blood, but I felt no pain. The swirls were still again. The strands of black, silver, and gold were in exactly the same position as before over the impossible red. Just as I remembered it. I seized Zaffirah's bag and put the amulet back where I'd found it. I didn't want to see it again.

"Isra sad. Can help?" I recognized Dearg's broken speech. He'd come back, and for the first time, I wasn't overjoyed to see him.

"You can't help now! Where were you when she was being taken away? Why didn't you help then?" I shouted.

Dearg retreated a few steps. I had never shouted at him like that before, and I expected him to thoughtlessly poof away as he always did. But he didn't this time. He stared at me with his yellow, bulbous eyes. "Sorry," he said finally. "Can help. Come. I show you."

He held out his left hand and mimicked my hand holding his with the other. I understood and pressed my palm into his. "Isra got amulet?" he asked.

"You knew about the amulet?" I felt the anger I had temporarily managed to silence rise inside me. He nodded nonchalantly while I trembled with fury.

"*Why didn't you tell me?*" I barked.

He shook his head slowly. "Couldn't. Good for Isra to find out by herself."

"Who are you to decide what's good for me and what's not?" I demanded.

"Isra must listen. Can help Isra find sister," Dearg growled.

"How?"

"Amulet."

I took the amulet out of the bag and passed it to Dearg. He put it in his mouth, bit it, swallowed it, and coughed it back out, dripping with his sticky saliva, but otherwise unharmed.

"Why did you do that?" I asked, slightly disgusted.

"To feel its . . . magic."

I narrowed my eyes and stared at him until he finally put the amulet down.

"Does Isra know where herself be?" he asked.

I looked around. Maybe I had gotten further away than I wanted. It was too dark to see. For God's sake, I was in a cave. I had no idea where I was. I hadn't seen a cave in my life.

"Where am I?" I asked.

Dearg would know the answer, but whether he chose to tell me was another matter. He hesitated before speaking. "Zarcane," he whispered finally. "Here." Dearg passed me the amulet and continued, "Isra must do what I did. Not safe for Isra to be here."

"I'm not going to bite the amulet, if that's what you want me to do."

"No, the words. Isra must repeat what I say, okay?"

I nodded, and he opened his mouth, pausing after each syllable. "Jeala. Umaa. Fae."

"No. The words are *Deala Roma Fae*. How do you think I got here?" I put the amulet on the ground and stepped away from it. *How hard can it be to work this thing?*

I yelled the words at the top of my lungs. "Deala Roma Fae!"

Nothing happened. I clenched my fists by my side. *What if I can't get out of here?*

"Again!" Dearg shouted.

I said the words softer this time. I focused on each syllable, making sure my lips formed the sound of every letter. The skin on my arms tingled before a blindingly white door of light appeared out of nowhere in the same place the amulet had been just seconds ago. I shivered, realizing that I was afraid. For the first time, I was afraid for myself, and not my mother or sister.

I didn't have long to think about that fear, though, because Dearg shoved me hard with his stone arms, and the white light engulfed me.

Eight

Farid

The bones in my knees clicked on collision with muscles and joints like clockwork, sounding every completed second. I wiped the sweat beading on my forehead.

Maya turned to look at me. She smiled, and then burst out laughing. Her high-pitched laugh was the sound of a hundred crickets chirping. It sure as hell was not beautiful or anything, but it was contagious. I echoed her earlier smile.

"What's so funny?" I asked.

"You are!" She opened her mouth wide and pointed at my forehead. "The night fell on you!" she said between giggles. She touched my hand, gesturing for me to look at it since she knew I couldn't see my own face

My hand was covered in the ashy black of my shoe polish can. I rubbed my forehead, trying to get the black off my face. Maya laughed harder. I sighed, realizing I was only spreading it.

"Oh come on, it's not that funny!" I grunted.

"It is!" she assured. I pressed my finger to her nose, turning it sooty like my hands. She frowned. "Heyyy!"

"I like you better with a black nose," I said, grinning. "It suits you."

I could see the white-domed top of the Basri shrine ahead, built on a hill, looking down upon us like an overprotective parent. The marble pillars, though dented, cracked, and fading, gave the shrine a certain elegance that didn't seem to belong in a dwelling so otherwise lacking. An uneven stone wall enclosed the tomb of the Sufi saint that had died there. There were no candles or fancy mirrors to distinguish it as a place of prayer. It was falling apart, but this was where Maya felt safest. This was where she slept. I couldn't exactly take a little girl I had found on the streets home to my parents, who were already struggling to feed me and my three brothers. No, they would not be welcoming in the least.

"You know I'm not tired." She picked at the dirt underneath her nail.

"Lies."

"I'm not!" She looked up this time, her eyes wide and serious. She had given up on her dirt-crusted nail.

"Okay, maybe you're not, but I am."

"Lies." She mimicked my low, grumbly voice. "Tell me a story, and I'll sleep. I promise."

"Fine. Come on."

She pulled out the tiny blue sleeping bag she had rammed into the small space in the stone wall the night before and laid it on the ground. It was ripped and faded. I should have bought her a new sleeping bag instead of shoes. She wouldn't have been as happy about it, but it would have kept her warmer at night. Children were like that. They didn't think about necessities, only about the pretty things. Her little dog nestled in beside her and nuzzled her neck.

"Which one do you want to hear?" I asked.

"I want one about princesses, dragons, and kings!" she cried happily.

"Okay," I sighed. "Are you ready?"

She nodded eagerly.

"Long ago . . .

Before there were buildings and cars and roads and traffic lights, there was a land far away. In this land, there lived creatures from story books. Fairies, elves, and mermaids—they were all there. But there was also a little human girl called Shay. Shay loved to go outside and play with these strange creatures. She even gave one of her dollhouses to her fairy friends.

One day, when Shay was out wandering, she came across a baby dragon. The dragon was crying, and he could hardly move. Shay picked up the dragon and brought him home. She spent many days nursing him back to health, but the poor dragon was never able to fly again. Having nowhere to go, he decided to stay with Shay.

Many years passed, and the dragon grew strong and fiery. He was very protective of Shay, and he followed her wherever she went. Shay lost all her friends because of this, as everyone in the land feared the big dragon. Word went out that the dragon was holding a damsel hostage and knights in shining armor came to slay him. But once they set their eyes upon the thick, scaly body of the dragon, they turned away. No knight was ever brave enough to face the fire-breathing dragon. But there was one man who eventually did and lived to tell the tale.

This man was a very unhappy man. He had journeyed through all the lands looking for something to make him smile again. When he heard about the dragon, he felt it was his duty to save the girl, and having nothing to live for anyway, he decided to try his luck. He arrived at Shay's door, armed with a sword that was almost taller than him. He broke the door down and the dragon was there, waiting.

"I have come to slay you, Dragon," he said. The poor man's hands were shaking as he said this, for the dragon was ten times his size and though he did not fear death, he did fear pain.

The dragon swatted him carelessly across the head like a pesky bug before Shay entered the room. Her eyes widened with fear as she took in the scene.

The moment this man set his eyes upon Shay, he smiled his first genuine smile in many long years, for Shay was the most beautiful woman he had ever seen.

"Please don't hurt my dragon," Shay said softly. Her voice was a lovely song to his ears.

"But is he not holding you prisoner?" the man asked, bewildered. His eyes never left Shay. Just as the smile never left his face.

She shook her head. "So many people fear him. No one comes to see me anymore. No one knows the truth. You are the first man I have spoken to in a long time. You see, I saved this dragon when he was a baby. He is my only friend now," Shay replied.

"I am sorry, my lady," he said, finally putting his sword on the ground. "I would love to be your friend, if you would have me. My name is Rafi."

Shay nodded, smiling. She hadn't had a new friend in a long time. Shay and Rafi became the closest of friends, and Rafi forgot all about his sadness. His journey had come to an end, and he had finally found what he was looking for in Shay—his happiness.

Rafi also told the world about the dragon and his broken wing that never truly healed. Instead of knights, doctors now traveled to see the dragon, in hopes of helping him fly once again.

"Did they fix his wing?" Maya asked.

I shrugged. "I hope they did."

"You don't know?"

I shook my head slowly.

"Well, I don't think they did. I think he was the last dragon in the world, and he wasn't able to fly and find a wife so the whole dragon race died out," Maya said nonchalantly.

"That's a little depressing."

She shrugged this time. "But it's the truth," she murmured.

Her eyelids, heavy with sleep, finally shut. I watched her for a while. Her skin was silver from the light of the crescent moon. She looked otherworldly. I couldn't bring myself to rise and leave, but I did eventually. I had to.

I was only a few meters away when I heard her scream. I knew it was her instantly. I ran as fast as my legs could take me. I was going to kill him. Whoever had touched Maya was going to die. I would knock his face in and feel his warm blood dripping down my arms.

Before I could get to the shrine, something cold and hard slapped me across the back of my head. My vision blurred and I fell. The pain was so severe I could no longer feel it. I forced my body to rise, but I couldn't, overcome with dizziness. A man stood over me.

"The more, the merrier, eh?" he said, laughing as he heaved me over his back.

Nine

Isra

"Isra, up. Up!" Dearg grumbled. He shook me and I blinked, trying to get my bearings. Dearg had pulled the sack around my body off my head, but my legs were still tangled in it. I peeled it away. I recognized the sack from last night, when the Snatchers had closed in on us. Wherever I had gone last night, I most definitely had not taken my body. The Snatchers must have just left me here when they realized I wasn't moving. I couldn't believe it. They had just left me in a dark alleyway to rot. I shook my head, trying to bring back the sanity I lost the night before.

"Come," Dearg instructed. I walked with him till we reached the downtown area once more.

Beggars and shoe shiners were taking their places, waiting for the affluents to come walking out with their heads held high and money bouncing with their pace in their carefully sewn pockets. I had only one thing on my mind, and that was to find my sister. Whatever trouble she was in, it was my fault.

"Please . . ."

"Sir, wait . . ."

"Ma'am, spare us some change . . ."

"Please . . ."

The beggars' words filled my ears within seconds. Few people with money stopped before the panhandlers. Even fewer parted with their money. Dearg squeezed my hand—a gesture of support that hurt and also felt meaningless. His hand was cold and hard in mine.

"Ask where Zaffirah," he mumbled in his gravelly voice. I did as he suggested, approaching a girl a little older than me.

"S'cuse me, I am looking for my sister. She's this tall." I raised my hand to my shoulder. "She's got dark, curly hair. Have you seen her? She was snatched last night." My voice shook, unintentionally, with desperation. The girl was with her own younger sister, holding her hand and subtly shielding her from any danger that I posed. How threatening could a sixteen-year-old, starving girl look?

"Who took her?" the younger girl chirruped.

The older one shook her head and hushed her sister. "There are many girls with dark, curly hair." She shrugged. I looked at the other children that stood close beside her. They had paused their begging to listen. I gave them a pleading look, but they too, shook their heads.

I knew that even if they did know, they wouldn't tell me. They had a saying here. Speak no evil, see no evil. People simply disappeared and that was it. They were erased from everyone's memory. It was worse than death; at least then, their existence was acknowledged. People still spoke of them, what they loved about them, what they hated. They were remembered as the people that they were—eternal in memory.

Hours passed. I asked everyone that I could. "Dearg, they don't know where she is. They don't know anything. They won't tell me!" I cried, frustrated.

He didn't answer. "Dearg?" I looked down at where Dearg was standing just seconds ago. He had *poofed* away . . . again. I didn't even have the emotional energy to be hurt by his insensitive act.

"Isra." I turned to look at the owner of the voice. She had hair as dark as raven's feathers and a strange look in her eyes. It wasn't the pity or sympathy that I had grown accustomed to in reply to my questions. It was something else. Support. Kindness . . . or so I liked to believe.

"Who are you? How do you know my name?" I asked. I folded my arms across my chest and studied her closely. I waited for her to answer, stunned that this girl was actually willing to help me.

The girl sensed my hesitation. "My name is Rhiya. Quick, you must come with me. I can help you find your sister."

The compulsion in her voice was hard to ignore. The girl seemed so sincere. I let my arms drop to my side and followed her. She led me into a dark, empty alleyway. Normally, following a stranger into a dingy alleyway was not something I would have done with such naïve obedience, but I was desperate. I was also certain I could fight this waif of a girl off if I had to.

"Okay, I need you to listen very carefully. Look to the right, and then quickly turn to the left. Blink, and tell me what you see." She must have seen the look of bewilderment painted on my face, because she was quick to add a pleading "please."

Deciding to humor her, I reluctantly did as she asked. I saw a house take shape before me. It was bigger than a cottage, but smaller than a mansion. Long, glass windows were set into the white cement of the walls.

"There is a house," I gasped, rubbing my eyes to make sure of its solidity.

"That's *my* house. Congratulations, you can see through the glamour. Come on." The girl sounded pleased with me, as though the dog she had been training finally learned how to do a trick. *I'm not your dog*, I thought with a scowl.

"What's glamour?" I asked, ignoring the smug tone of her voice.

"Well, it's kind of like a disguise, so that the ones without the *sight* can't see it."

"The *sight*?"

"Come inside. My mother will explain everything."

Rhiya turned the door handle and gestured for me to go in first. I noticed that the handle didn't have a keyhole. I supposed if your house had such a complicated method of being seen, then you didn't really need a lock.

"Rhiya, darling, were you able to find her?" I heard her mother call out as soon as the front door creaked shut behind us.

"I was, Mumma," Rhiya replied. She turned to me. "This way."

I followed her into a dark room lit only by the blue light of a small, spherical lamp.

"Here she is," Rhiya called out to the darkness.

It took a moment for my eyes to adjust, but when they did, I saw the gypsy woman immediately. Silvery strands of hair escaped from the jeweled scarf wrapped around her head and framed her pale, porcelain face. A formidable air of wisdom surrounded her and made her look years beyond her age. Her eyes were what called my attention. They glowed, a sparkling violet matching the feathers hanging from her ears, but they were unable to focus on anything. She was blind.

"Hello?" I mumbled, annoyed at all the mystery.

"Isra," she gasped. "Come. Sit down. You have your mother's voice—"

"You knew my mother?" I asked.

"I did. You were blessed, my dear, to have—"

"Were," I murmured. *Past tense.* "You know." I was shocked. A day had passed since we ran away, and yet this woman knew what had happened to my mother. Why had I never seen her before today?

She nodded. "She knew me as Calliel. I know more than you think, but even so, I'm not the one you should be afraid of."

Questions swam in my head. There were so many that I couldn't focus on one to bring to my lips. I remained silent. Calliel gave me a knowing smile, as if she could read my mind. It was a smile that was so strangely comforting, it instantly put me at ease and seized my trust. I struggled to hold on to my questions.

"Rhiya!" Calliel called. I looked around. Though I hadn't heard her leave, the girl was gone. Seconds passed before she once again appeared in the doorway.

"Yes, Mumma." She approached Calliel.

"*Jaanu,* have you readied her room?" she asked, gently combing the girl's hair.

"I have. Come, I'll show it to you," Rhiya said, gesturing for me to stand and follow her out.

"Wait, my sister . . . you said you would help me!"

"We'll talk later. Go now, you must be exhausted."

Reluctantly, I stood and trailed after the girl. She kept up a mindless chatter of useless information while she led me up the wooden stairs and then to a room on the left.

"What do you think?" she asked, finally letting me speak. The door that she'd pushed open revealed a cramped, but homey, well-lit room. The walls were a pale cream and dappled in places with paint chips. A bookshelf protruded from the wall beside the bed, filled with a number of trinkets and books. More books than I had ever seen before in one place.

Hanging on the back wall was a clock that reminded me of the one my father had once brought home. It had had a round, wooden face. It was broken when my father found it, but he'd fixed it and given it to me—a present on my birthday. He'd taught me how to read it too. I'd loved the curved, black numbers and the endless, tranquil ticking. Sometimes, when I couldn't sleep, I would listen to it until exhaustion finally hit me. Zaffirah and my mother had hated its monotonous ticking. I'd begged and begged for her not to sell it away, but we needed the money.

As always, sell to survive. Her motto, I thought.

"It's lovely," I replied. My voice sounded flat to my ears.

She nodded, unfazed. "There are clothes in the cupboard." She pointed to the two wooden doors. "Bathroom's on the right. My room is across the hall, if you need me. We'll be having dinner soon. You should change and shower." She left, shutting the door quietly behind her. It didn't creak in protest, but obediently shut at Rhiya's touch.

I collapsed onto the bed and shut my eyes. Sleep didn't come, however much I wanted it to. My head was too full of confused thoughts. A room like this would once have impressed me to no end, but now, I couldn't care less. I felt nothing but an overwhelming sadness at having no one to share it with.

I got up and opened the cupboard. Strips of cotton, silk, and polyester instantly brushed my face. I ran my fingers through the soft fabrics, finally stopping at a simple, white *shalwaar kameez.* I pulled the outfit off the hanger.

Carrying it in my hand, I made my way to the bathroom. It was strangely built, with a glass chamber, a huge white sink, and a fancy toilet. I stepped through the glass and turned the tap on. I placed my hand under the facet, and boiling water seared my skin. I yelped with pain and turned it off. When I turned on the second tap, glacial water splashed my face. I shivered and turned that one off too. I had never felt water so hot or cold. The water I showered with in my slum was water from the canal that ran outside my home. We kept that water in a bucket and though it was a little cold, it was much warmer than this. There was no third tap.

I wondered how I could make the water temperature comfortable. I turned both the taps on, hoping that the water wouldn't be too cold or too hot. A drop of warm water hit my skin. My neck arched back as more drops fell. They trickled down my back like phantom fingers tracing my spine. We didn't have showers like this at home. I washed the soapy suds off my body, peeling layer after layer of dirt off my skin. Smelling of vanilla and coconut, I wrapped the towel hanging behind the door around me.

"This is where we eat," Rhiya informed. In the middle of the dining room was a beautifully crafted, cherry wood table. Eight chairs were tucked into its edges. Calliel occupied the one on the far end of the room.

"Come, sit down. I bet you're hungry." Calliel gestured. *Starving actually*, I thought. I walked over to the seat adjacent to Calliel. Rhiya sat across from me. As soon as we were seated, a grey stone creature dressed in a plain white apron walked into the room with a silver tray in his hand. I stared at him as he placed a glass jug, filled with orange water, on the table.

"Dearg?" I asked. The creature shook his head.

"I'm sorry, miss, my name's not Dearg," he said gruffly.

"Have you seen a traveler before?" Rhiya asked, curiously.

"What's a traveler?" I questioned.

"Well, our Corom is a traveler," Calliel replied.

"They're the only creatures that can pass between lands even when the borders are locked. They belong to both worlds. They advise and serve anyone magical really," Rhiya piped in.

I didn't bother trying to make sense of her words. There wasn't a need to. "Well . . . I knew a creature like him. I've known him ever since I was born."

"The sightless can't see them, you know."

"I'm sorry, the sightless? You mean . . ." I glanced at Calliel.

"No, not blind," Rhiya quipped, laughing at me.

"What are the sightless, then?" I retorted.

"You know . . . the normal humans."

"Rhiya, hush," Calliel chided.

"I was just telling her—"

"We will talk about it later," Calliel said.

I didn't say anything. Instead, I focused my eyes on the little creature. He approached the table and placed two dishes in front of me. I looked at the pot filled to its brim with colored rice grains. Rice that my family had stopped buying because we could no longer afford it. Inside, I saw meat clinging to wing bones. The spicy smell of fragrant rice mingled with the herbal scent of the tender chicken within it. Beside the pot was a bowl of clean-cut vegetables. I felt my mouth water, almost forgetting about what Rhiya had just blurted.

"Here, take some biryani. It's her best dish," Rhiya gushed, as she attempted to change the subject. She had taken Calliel's rebuking seriously. Looking at her mother, she passed me the pot of rice.

"Thank you," I murmured. I had never seen so much food in my life before. I scooped a small serving onto my plate.

"Take more," Calliel said. She took the spoon from my hands and dolloped a piece of chicken onto my plate.

The utensils were new to me. I gripped them clumsily between my forefinger and thumb, trying to look as though it wasn't the first time I was using them. I used my knife to cut through the chicken. It came away easily on my fork. I lifted the fork to my mouth, automatically leaning in to take a bite. I couldn't remember the last time I had tasted chicken, or any meat for that matter. My teeth sank into the flesh. I spooned the golden rice into my mouth. The exotic combination of the spices and herbs sparked life into my taste buds.

"It's . . . delicious," I said between mouthfuls.

"I'm glad you think so," Calliel answered.

I sipped the glass of orange juice that had been placed beside my plate. The sugary liquid filled my mouth. I wiped my lips clean and asked the question that had been on my mind ever since I heard Rhiya call my name. The food had only served as a temporary distraction.

"Rhiya told me you knew who took my sister. So . . . who was it? How do I find her?"

"She what? Rhiya!" Calliel scolded. A shocked look was painted over her face. Rhiya was shaking her head vigorously, gesturing for me to be quiet. That was all I needed to see to know that they didn't, in fact, know more than I did about the whereabouts of my sister.

"I'm sorry I lied, Isra, but you had only one thing on your mind—"

"Why did you bring me here if you didn't know anything about my sister?" I interrupted. "I take up room. I eat your food. Why am I here?"

"It really doesn't matter," Calliel answered, calmly.

"Why am I here?" I repeated the question.

"I promised I would protect you."

"To who? What are you supposed to be? My bodyguard? Protect me from what? I don't need protection!" My voice gradually got louder. "My sister did! Why didn't you protect her?"

"Did your mother not tell you anything?" Rhiya asked.

"Clearly not. She didn't tell me she knew you. She didn't tell me about any of this, and I don't care what she did or did not tell me, because right now, all I want is my sister back!" I shouted, finally losing control.

"Isra, there is no need to yell. We'll do our best to find her.

That's all I can promise. We'll go to a police station tomorrow," Calliel said. She got up and strode out of the room. The rice, vegetables, and chicken were left on her plate, half eaten. The door slid shut behind her.

"I'm sorry," Rhiya whispered. "It's my fault. Don't be angry at her."

I shook my head and narrowed my eyes at her. "I'm going to bed," I muttered.

My appetite was gone. The sight of food on the table was making me want to vomit. I walked out of the room with thoughts of Zaffirah in my head, leaving Rhiya behind.

Pushing the door to my borrowed room open, I raced to the comfort of the bed. The bed lowered with my weight, almost touching the ground. I pulled the blankets close around my body and felt the lids of my eyes fall shut, hoping that, at least in my dreams, I could be with my sister, but even that was too much to ask.

Instead, my white wings unfolded and thumped to the simple rhythmic beat of my heart. *One, two. One, two. One, two.* I was free. I stooped low, falling. At the last second, I turned up and my body rose in a steady ascent into the clouds. I looked down at the cherry blossom trees and flowers below me. Fluttering just above them were multi-colored butterflies, yellow bumble bees and other airborne creatures I had no name for as of yet.

I caught sight of a dark disarray of hair. It was a little girl. She bent her head to smell a budding rose. I called to her. "Hey!"

She turned instantly. It was Maya. Her eyes were round disks as she stared at me. She held up her hands, palms up. "Help me," she murmured. "Please, help me."

My eyes opened, the dream a distant memory.

Ten

Farid

"Let me go!" I yelled. It was hard to keep my voice from shaking. Rough laughter filled the air, drowning out my shout.

"Shut up!" a man grunted. He elbowed me in the space between my ribs, as if to emphasize the point.

My knees hit the ground as the sack that had been pulled over my head was tossed away. Cool air surrounded me. Greedily gulping it in, I knew I would never take fresh air for granted again. They had brought me to a grey room. The only color came from a flickering yellow light above me, casting large shadows on the walls. The room was empty save for a single piece of furniture—a desk. *Where is Maya?* Behind the desk, a man set down his bubbling glass of beer. His eyes were bloodshot and glassy.

He raised his finger to his lips. "Shushhhh," he slurred.

I scrambled to my feet, moving as far away from the man as I possibly could, only stopping short of cowering in the corner. He eyed me from the topmost strand of my hair to the dirt caked under the soles of my feet. His tongue stuck out, and he licked the shimmering drops of beer from his lips.

"Would you like a sip, boy? This here is good stuff." He grinned, showing off his yellow, decaying teeth. They looked like twisted rocks covered with mold, clinging to the soft flesh of his gums.

I didn't shake my head. A shrill scream from another room punctured the silence. *Is that Maya?* The man pressed his fingers in his ears and began singing tunelessly to himself, a lackluster song that I couldn't recognize. When the screaming finally subsided to a weak moan, the man looked around suspiciously before his eyes fell upon me once more.

"Let me tell you a secret," he whispered. "I hate it when they scream. If you be a good little boy and don't yell—that child sounded mad, didn't she? Completely cuckoo! If you don't yell, I pinkie promise I won't hurt you . . . not on purpose, boy. You see, sometimes I have these *impulses.* Then I can't help it. You understand, don't you?" His eyes bored into mine. I noticed the pale, milky quality of his right eye. It almost looked as though it had a thin layer of skin growing over it.

"Where's Maya?" I asked, my voice steely and my eyes narrowed. He stared back, smiling. I wanted to rip that smile from his face. I was fairly certain I could, but then more men would come and punish me for it. I'd lose a hand or a leg, and this man would only lose his smile.

The man rose from behind the table. The screech of his chair reverberated off the walls and into my ears. He walked toward me. I moved back, and before I knew it, I had pressed myself into the wall with such force, the bones in my back began to ache. A shiver shuddered through my body, and I clamped my fist in my mouth to stifle the volume of a yell that was bubbling from the pit of my stomach. *Stop it*, I chided. *You're not afraid. Look at him. You could kill him in a fight.*

The man put his thick hands on my shoulders and exhaled on my face. His breath stank of heavy booze and onions. I flinched. "Who? We took many little girls last night," he whispered. The smile never left his face, but there was something off about it. It wasn't a happy smile. His fingers squeezed my shoulder blades until I cried out in pain.

He laughed and flicked a stray strand of hair away from my face. "I'm sure you'll find a little girl of your liking to be with you soon, but first, you have to promise to be a good boy. I'm your daddy now." He leaned in closer, his pinkie finger dancing in the air.

"You know it doesn't count if you don't pinkie swear." He laughed. The man's eyes brightened as he grabbed my finger. His pinkie tightened around mine and I heard it snap. My finger throbbed in agony. I couldn't move it. I couldn't feel anything but the pain.

The man's hands dropped to his side, and he nodded solemnly. I rubbed my finger, already noticing the red blossoming over it as it swelled. "Good. Now please, call me *Daddy*," he slurred. He dragged his feet back to his chair and picked up his glass.

"Would you like a sip, boy?" he asked.

Eleven

Isra

"I understand ma'am, but you see, we can't do anything about it if you can't tell us what the kidnapper
looked like."

Calliel had taken me to the police station, but I knew
the whole search for Zaffirah would be hopeless if the officer
couldn't get a good description of the men that had kidnapped
her. I squeezed the amulet I'd stuffed into my pocket. I couldn't
bear to be apart from it anymore, knowing the power it held. I
wished with all my heart that I could help my sister. It was my

fault. I wished that I could change the past. That I could draw the police officer a picture.

As soon as that thought came into my mind, my hand suddenly began itching for a pencil. I opened my mouth and words I hadn't even had time to think of flew out of my mouth.

"S'cuse me, sir, do you have a piece of paper and a pencil? I can show you what the man looked like," I interrupted.

The police officer gave Calliel a questioning look and she nodded, telling the officer to do as I asked.

"Here." He handed me the paper and pencil. I took it, hoping desperately that I knew what I was doing.

The pencil in my hand kissed the piece of paper as it began to form marks. I shaded in the grooves and creases that the face had. As a child, I had never been an artist. I couldn't draw. Stick men were a great achievement for me, but the face I had just drawn—it was something that should have taken extraordinary talent. It should have . . . but it didn't. My hand, with a mind of its own, finished off the sketch and returned to my control. I used the blunt end of the pencil and pointed at the drawing.

"This is what he looked like," I said, confidence coating my voice.

The police officer gaped in awe. When he recovered from the surprise I had given him, he put on his glasses and took a closer look at the picture. Seconds passed before he finally spoke.

"We know his kind; there are a lot of them in Islamabad, but this guy—" He stabbed the almost photographic image I had drawn with his pen. "I have seen him before. I assure you that he will be caught."

I swallowed the lump in my throat. The officer's eyes had turned cold. I hoped he was thinking of all the ways he could brutally kill this man. It was comforting to know my hatred for Zaffirah's kidnappers was, in that moment, completely shared.

"Thanks for your time, Constable," Calliel said; her sugar-coated voice was syrupy. We both got up in sync and walked out of the police station.

I walked outside much happier; but unexpectedly, even that happiness dulled as I set my eyes upon Ammun. He looked different, but I was sure it was him. His hair was washed, clean of the small, brown beads that had clung to each one of his thin strands when I had first seen him. He was dressed in a new pair of clothes, also completely spotless. He looked just like one of the rich men—an affluent. I blinked to make sure I wasn't imagining it. I rubbed my eyes as he came closer.

Quickening his pace, he shouted, "Isra, I'm sorry, please listen to me. Isra!"

I ran blindly. I could hear Calliel's cries over Ammun's, but all I could think about was getting as far away from the boy as I could. I could feel the scorching, venomous fury throb through my veins. I hated him . . . almost as much as the men who had kidnapped Zaffirah. We were only there because of him, and now, Zaffirah was gone. For all I knew, he could have set us up. Sold us to the Snatchers for a few bucks. Was that how he got those nice clothes? *I can't believe I trusted him.*

His footsteps hit the ground close behind me. It wouldn't be long before he caught me. I could feel the familiar cramping in my stomach as my heart gained speed with every step and then suddenly, the blackness was back. I was fainting. Again.

I opened my eyes what seemed like days later, but the sight of the sun outside my window told me that only a couple of hours had passed. I stared at the faultless, eggshell-white ceiling, clear of cracks. The clean, minty smell of antiseptic was suffocating. My body was tucked carefully into a matching white blanket, and my head rested on a thick pillow. I caught sight of my hand; a needle was inserted deep into my wrist. It attached to a loud and constantly beeping machine. My hand automatically tugged at the needle. Panic rushed through me when I realized I couldn't untangle myself from the contraption. *Where am I?*

I saw Ammun with his head bent and a pencil in his right hand. He was clutching a piece of paper with a drawing. A face, maybe. I couldn't tell. He looked up. It was definitely a face. He crumpled it into his fist.

"Hey, you're awake! I came looking for you—I was late—you weren't there—I'm sorry. I came back, though. What happened?" Ammun got up from his seat. A string of words rushed out of his mouth. He sincerely looked sorry.

"Get this off my hand," I croaked.

"You're in a hospital—that thing connected to you, it's an IV, and that other machine, it monitors your heart rate. You need to relax," he said.

I stared at him for a long time. "Do you know where Zaffirah is?" I pronounced each word carefully, measuring my words.

Ammun didn't shake his head, but he didn't reply either. An awkward silence filled the space between us. A few seconds passed and still he remained soundless. I thought I wasn't going to get an answer until he finally spoke. A soft, worried reply.

"Wasn't she with you? I looked around after you . . . you know . . . passed out. I couldn't find her." He paused. "But we'll go back together and look for her. Don't worry." He rushed the last two sentences. They were meant to be reassuring.

"Would I be asking if I knew? There's no point in looking for her. A Snatcher grabbed her last night. She's gone."

Silence. I rolled over in my bed so I could turn away from him and face the window instead. Tears were threatening to fall out of my eyes. I held them back, my eyes stinging. I wouldn't let him see me cry.

Just at that moment, Calliel burst through the door. I turned to look at her. Her blind eyes were wide and searching. The tension in her posture instantly faded as she sensed rather than *saw* me. Her unseeing eyes passed over me and stopped to look at Ammun. His head jerked up, and he placed his body protectively between Calliel and the bed on which I was lying. My mouth opened to explain the woman's presence, but she cut me off before even a letter slipped from my lips.

"It is not me you should be protecting her from," she said in a sharp voice. Ammun looked at me, clearly waiting for an explanation.

"Her name is Calliel. She is helping me find Zaffirah," I said in answer to his glare. "It would be great if you would stop scowling at her. She's done more for me than you ever did, or will," I snapped.

I thought I saw him flinch at my harsh tone, but he was so quick to regain his composure that I wondered if maybe I had imagined it. He looked at her from head to toe before speaking.

"I see," he said at last.

Calliel stepped into the room, shutting the door behind her. "You are welcome to—"

"No." Ammun held up his hand. "Isra, I'm sorry. I didn't mean for you to lose Zaffirah. I hope you believe me when I say that. I'm going now."

Ammun turned on his heel and walked toward the door. As he left, my hatred also departed and guilt replaced it. What happened had not been Ammun's fault entirely, I realized. Part of the blame was my own, for bringing my sister into the darkness of the alleyways, where men like the Snatchers always lurked. I was stupid. I wasn't thinking, and now my sister's life was in danger.

I almost leapt out of the bed, held back only by the tubes connected to my body. Calliel gently pushed me back into the pillow.

"Stay. You need to rest. I'll go talk to him," she said. As I watched her leave the room, I forced myself to stop from going after her.

Minutes passed before Calliel finally returned. "He'll be back tomorrow."

Twelve

Farid

"Get up, boy. We're leaving."

The man yanked me to my feet. His grimy nails pressed into my arm. I didn't know how long I had been here. The room I was in had the windows barred shut, blocking any light that would have shone through otherwise. There were other children here too. So many of them that I lost count. I hated numbers.

I tried looking for Maya, but she wasn't here. I hummed quietly as the children cried for their mothers and their fathers.

Some of them had shrill screams of fear that sounded more like the calls of wild animals rather than a child. I could still hear the muffled sobs of other children as they tried to sleep away their pain. The older ones did their best to comfort the younger ones, but I could tell that they made terrible substitutes for their actual parents.

"What are you waiting for?" The man's eyebrows knitted together and the corners of his lips turned downward as he frowned. Seconds passed as he waited for an answer.

I yawned, opening my jaw as wide as a cat's. "I think I'll just sleep here, thank you," I muttered.

The girl beside me, who had been sleeping when I got here and was somehow still sleeping, woke up and caught sight of the man. *Why does she look so familiar?* She shouted, using all the breath that her lungs contained. She shouted with the fear of an animal in the clutches of its predator, awaiting death. The man grabbed the small, curly-haired girl and slapped her across the face. She fell to her knees, and then there was silence. For a moment, all the cries halted and the children retreated to the far corners of the room. The man grinned like a lunatic and raised his fingers to his lips.

"Shushhh," he whispered. His voice traveled across the room, a silent, dangerous warning. He had made his point and now the children didn't dare to let out even a whimper.

"You won't be getting any sleep here, boy. Come with me. I won't hurt you as long as you keep your promise. You'll do that, won't you?"

"Actually, I'm all right here."

"Don't be silly, boy!" He let out a loud laugh and the children around me flinched.

"Really, I'm okay." As soon as the words had come out of my mouth, I knew I shouldn't have said them. The man's eyes narrowed to slits.

"You will not disobey your father."

His hand slid around my neck, cupping my face in his clammy palms. Then, ever so slowly, his grip began to tighten until I couldn't breathe anymore. I coughed and pried at his fingers. My eyes began to water. From the corner of my eye, I saw the small, curly-haired girl approach the man. The girl kicked him in the groin with all the strength that she could muster.

The man's hands instantly fell from my neck, and he shrank to the ground in pain. With the darkness distorting her, I saw the girl wait to see the result of her handiwork and smile at its effectiveness. It was a cruel smile that didn't belong on a face I knew would be innocent. Her eyes flashed. I chased after her. She stopped only for a second before running toward the door. She was a fast runner. My legs ached trying to keep up with her.

Then suddenly, out of nowhere, arms tightened around my stomach and lifted me up. I felt hot, stale breath in my ear and instantly I knew that the man had gotten up and chased us down . . . well, one of us at least.

"That was a bad thing you did, boy. Very bad. You almost broke your promise. Now, you'll see what happens to the bad boys in our home."

Thirteen

Isra

I looked at the large, green tree that stood outside my window. Its plethora of leaves ranged from the brightest jade to the sharpest yellow. The birds had used it to create a nesting home. I watched as a mummy bird gently nudged her babies out of the nest. I saw one fall from the tree. Seconds passed and I thought it would die, but then I saw the baby soar high above the ground into the infinite spread of the sky. I gazed longingly at the bird's feathered wings expanding and recoiling with the current of the wind. The creature flew like an aerial torpedo to its safe haven in the giant tree.

Ammun had left a couple of hours ago. His face had given away nothing, but his tone couldn't mask the hurt and anger he felt.

"Isra, I spoke to the doctors, and they've said you can leave tomorrow. Just please don't worry me like that again. You're under my care now," Calliel reprimanded; her voice still contained traces of the concern that had been expressed on her face before. She sounded almost like my mother.

"I'm sorry, I wanted to get away from him."

"I know, child, I know. It's not his fault. We'll find her."

I nodded. "I miss her."

My body shook with sadness as the tears I had been holding back finally escaped. Calliel put her arms around me and gently stroked my hair back. I found myself leaning into her until my sobs finally subsided.

"I had a sister too," Calliel said, when I had stopped crying. The trails that my tears left behind dried on my cheeks.

"What was she like?" I asked.

"She was beautiful. Her voice was warm and smooth like milk. Rhiya's is like that too."

"What happened to her?"

"She changed," Calliel answered abruptly. Her reply was firm and tight-lipped. I sensed that she wanted nothing more said on that subject. I wondered why she had brought it up to begin with.

"I'm sorry, I didn't mean to pry."

She waved off my apology as though it was nothing. "I brought you something," she informed with a smile. I watched her hands dip into the cerulean purse at her side. They came out holding a leather-bound notebook.

"What is it?"

"It was your mother's, and now, it is yours." She placed the book on the table beside my bed. "I'll come back with Rhiya tomorrow. They want to make sure you're all right before they release you. Get some rest. Good night, Isra," Calliel said as she leaned in to comfort me with a silent hug, before standing up.

"Wait," I said.

Calliel turned.

"Where did you get this?"

"I'm sure your mother must have thought she lost it. I never had the chance to give it back to her, so I'm giving it to you, instead."

"Thank you," I mumbled.

I watched the door shut behind her and picked up the book she had left. My fingers traced the title: *The Keeper's Diary*. It was carved into the tanned leather cover of the thick book. The strange, musty smell tickled the inside of my nose. My fingers floated to the right hand corner of the book. I urged them down, forcing the cover to flip over, but there it stayed. Tightly in place. The book was locked—jammed shut. I searched around, feeling for a keyhole. There was none. My index finger stopped at a circular indentation in the fore edge of the book. The indentation was made on a thick binding of the same tanned leather. I pulled it and tugged it, but it didn't budge. The binding was stronger than it looked.

Fourteen

Farid

As useless as kicking and yelling out was, I couldn't stop. I was trapped, but I didn't want to believe it. The man twisted my arms behind me, murmuring incomprehensible words as he did so. He smiled, seeming to be comforted by my silent jerks of pain. He tied my wrists together with a coarse piece of rope. His fingers were nimble and experienced. They worked quickly with little hesitation. He had done this so many times before that now, he didn't even need to think about which end went under which loop;

his fingers knew out of habit. He must have tied so many children before me—so many children who had probably faced their inevitable demise and were now gone from this world. I was next. I was dead. And no one would ever know. I would silently disappear. My parents would miss the money I earned, I'm sure, but they wouldn't miss me.

His hands curled around my arm, and his dirty fingernails broke through my skin. Blood trailed down my arm, past his fingers, to my elbow and even further still. He knelt down and produced another rope. This one was intended for my ankles.

"Don't you dare move, boy," he hissed into my ear.

With a simple flick of his palms, he pushed me to the floor. The cold tiles sent a shiver down my spine. I didn't say a word. I wouldn't beg this man.

He knelt down beside me, his eyes glowing dark with insanity. He yanked my feet together and wrapped the rope over my ankles. A shrill shriek broke out from somewhere in the house. I hoped it wasn't the girl that had run away with me, but the scream had come from her direction. It filled the silence. The man's head snapped around. He'd lost interest in me. He looked up, then to the side, then the other. He repeated the motions. His oily hair, though not long, flew as he jerked from side to side.

He hadn't tied the rope yet. I peeled it off my ankles and rose as quietly as I could. I crept back, tiptoeing almost, silently praying that he wouldn't see me.

"Oi!" he yelled. "Where you going, boy? Did I say you could leave?" His breathing was labored. Sweat fell from his temples and dripped down the side of his face, sticking strands of his hair to his skin. He shook his head wildly.

"Where are you going, boy?" he sang out again.

I looked behind me. There was a corridor—dark, but spacious enough that I could run through it. What other choice did I have? I made up my mind, turning on the balls of my feet. I took a deep breath and ran as fast as my legs would allow me—as fast as my heart was beating. I ran. Faster than I had ever run before. I almost thought that I had gotten away. That was my mistake. That second in which I paused to take a breath was enough. He caught me and gave me no mercy. He grabbed my legs, tackled me to the ground, and from the back pocket of his trousers, he pulled out a gun.

Fifteen

Farid

The metal of the gun reflected the white light above me. It was blinding. I rubbed my palms together. They were wet, coated with a thick layer of sweat. I stared at the man. His lips were slightly curled up with a knowing expression. He *knew* he had the power to end my life right there and then, and I couldn't see any reason why he wouldn't.

"You've been a very bad boy," he whispered.

He shoved the gun toward my head, the cold metal burning a ring of fire on my forehead. I flinched. I was going to die. There was nothing I could do. I thought I could beat him. I was wrong. His finger stroked the trigger, and he hummed his tuneless melody. My body quivered with fear. I would never see Maya again. I would never see my stupid brothers. I would never see anyone. Ever. Again. I pressed my eyelids shut. If he wanted to kill me, he could go right ahead. I wasn't about to plead for a life so useless.

"Goodbye, boy."

There was a silent click. I gasped. My body collapsed. He tucked the gun under his belt.

"No need for so much drama, boy. I'm not a killer. Plus, you'll bring me so much money . . . when you lose a hand or maybe a leg?" He grinned, enjoying the way I squirmed. He tossed me over his shoulder. I curled my fingers into fists and rammed them into his back. I yelled at the top of my lungs. My shout was deafening, even in my own ears, but the man was suddenly immune to it all.

He carried me outside. There was another man there. Lying limp in his arms was the girl with curly hair. Her face was turned away. *She's unconscious, that's all*, I told myself. *Look, you can see her breathing.*

The glowing sun pierced the darkness of the night. Its fingers stretched across the sky—brighter than ever. Beside the house was a truck. The other man got in the back with the girl while I was shoved into the passenger seat. The man reached into his pocket and produced an injection filled with a yellow liquid. He uncapped the needle and stretched out my arm. I pulled away, kicking. I tried to punch him, but it was useless. The man held me down, and the needle went deep into my skin, despite my efforts. I wasn't used to being so powerless. Every fight that I had ever been in, I had won. But here I was, losing when it truly mattered.

"Sleep tight, boy."

My vision went blurry. I reached out to steady myself, but I couldn't grip anything. The colors mixed into one. My head throbbed in agony, and the world seemed to grow a little darker and more lifeless.

"No . . ." I murmured.

Sixteen

Isra

"Isra! Wake up! They found her!" Rhiya shook my shoulders. Her low, muffled voice gently pulled me back to Earth. She put her arm around me and helped me out of the bed. It took me a while to register what Rhiya was saying.

"They found Zaffirah!" she said again.

"They found her . . ." I repeated to myself. "They found her? How?" I asked, louder this time.

"They caught her kidnappers, as well. There were two of them; they were both found in a car accident. One of them was pronounced dead on the spot, but they put the other one in a cell. Zaffirah survived. She's alive! But she suffered a head injury. A metal fragment from the car grazed her head," Rhiya answered. My jaw dropped. "She's alive . . . but . . . she's in a coma," Rhiya continued.

The last word bounced around in my head. *Coma coma coma coma.* I didn't know whether Rhiya was still talking. All I could hear was the word "*coma.*" It slammed against the walls of my skull, ricocheting back and forth. I could feel the cold metal hands of despair tighten around my neck. A wave of nausea washed over me as fat, salty drops clouded my eyes. I tried to reason with myself. At least she wasn't dead. There was a chance she might be able to hear me and see me. At least she was still alive.

"Isra! Snap out of it!" Rhiya shouted. She snapped her fingers in my face, interrupting my inner quarrel.

"I want to see her," I said at last.

"I know," Rhiya replied. "Come on." She tugged at my arm, helping me off the bed.

I walked out of the hospital room with Rhiya. Calliel was waiting outside, her arms crossed. Her eyes lit up as she sensed my presence, or maybe Rhiya's. I could never understand how she did that.

"She just came out of the emergency room," she informed.

"Where is she?"

"I'll take you to her."

I walked slowly, concentrating on putting my left leg down, and then my right. Left, right, left, right. The steady tapping of my feet hitting the ground did little to calm me. I was scared to see her in the way Rhiya had told me I would. I tried to convince myself that I wasn't, but I knew the truth, smoldering undyingly into the back of my brain. We stopped just in front of her door. Everything was a foggy mist in my head.

"I need to do this alone," I said.

Calliel stepped away from me. I suppose she was expecting me to walk right into Zaffirah's room, but I stayed where I was; as if the ground had suddenly come alive and chained my ankles to the tiles on the floor.

What is wrong with me? She was my sister. She needed me. I should have been in there with no hesitation at all. If the roles were reversed, that's all I would have asked from her. Wouldn't I? My last thought wiped away all my hesitations. I pushed the handle down gently and walked into her room.

She was lying on the bed as I had expected, in a deep sleep. Her face was pallid, and her body was tucked carefully under the blanket. I pulled the chair from the corner of the room and set it down, close to her bed.

"Zaffirah, please come back," I whispered. My hand found hers. I squeezed it tightly, but her's remained limp in mine. "Zaffirah, if you can hear me, please come back."

I held back the tears, but I could feel my attempts failing. I got up, turned away from Zaffirah and walked to the window. I pulled it open, letting the air from outside into the room. I was still not used to having the air conditioner on. I preferred the fresh air to the frozen, stale air the air conditioner produced. I looked outside. The darkness of the night almost blinded my vision.

I looked at the two tiny stars shining in the sky and remembered what my mother used to say about shooting stars: *if you ever see one, make a wish, and never doubt that it will come true.* Where did a shooting star hide when you really needed one?

"Isra, turn around," said the tinkling, bell-like voice of my sister from behind me.

Seventeen

Farid

All I saw was wings. Black and silver wings. They came out of nowhere and enveloped me. Suddenly, I was flying. Away from the wreckage of the truck and the crushed, bloody body in the driver's seat. My head throbbed with a pain that made it hard to breathe. None of the injuries I had suffered in fights could compare to this. It was all over my body—in the spaces between my joints and on the surface of my skin. I closed my eyes and drifted in and out of consciousness.

Moments later, fingers pried open my mouth, and a bitter liquid was poured down my throat. I coughed part of it out; it stained the floor a yellowish-brown. My hand came away from my head red and sticky with blood.

I was on a dirty couch in a dingy apartment, minimally furnished. The pale wallpaper was peeling, and the floor was littered with cigarette butts and empty packets of God knew what.

"Get up, you're okay." I looked up at the boy before me. He didn't have wings or anything. He was just a boy with a pink scar and a crooked nose. Older than me by several years. He held out a hand and brought me to my feet. He was taller and stronger too. I could tell by how easily he had pulled me up.

"Who are you?" I asked.

"Not who . . . the word you are look for is *what*." He grinned a manic smile. *When did the world get so full of crazy nut jobs?* He looked meaningfully at me and repeated, "*What* am I?"

Eighteen

Isra

I turned around, slowly shifting my feet. Zaffirah was out of the bed. The machines that I had seen attached to her wrist were pushed to the other side of the room. She was standing up straight, and the ashen look her face had had on before was gone. In her hand was a yellowish thread. The amulet hung at the bottom, swinging like a pendulum. The black, red, silver, and gold were swirling around each other. Just like the day it had saved me from being kidnapped. I gasped. It took a couple of seconds for the shock to really hit.

My sister was okay again. She was moving. Not in a coma, but literally moving. I ran to hug her, holding her tight in my arms. I didn't ever want to let her go. Was it the amulet that brought her back? I kissed her softly on the cheek, my arms still around her. She started to pull away.

"Isra, I have to show you something," she said. Her voice was steady and knowing.

She opened her hand and placed the amulet on the ground. I watched in silence as her eyelids fell, blocking the view of her brown eyes. She was on her knees now; she brought the palm of her right hand into contact with the amulet and the room filled with the same burning scent that had first met my nose when we were about to run away. I saw the flicker of flames that licked my sister's fingers, but she didn't notice. Her face was cold in concentration as she whispered the magic words:

"Deala Roma Fae."

I knew what she was expecting, but nothing happened. The white doorway didn't appear. *Why is everyone always trying to teach me what to do?*

My hands automatically reached out for the amulet on the floor. Zaffirah didn't even need to pass it to me. It floated toward me as though it was a small piece of iron attracted to the magnet of my hand. Zaffirah opened her eyes, but her face was blank. I knelt to the ground like Zaffirah had done seconds ago.

"Let me try," I said, smiling. "Deala Roma Fae."

Lightning flashed through the room and threads of white light tied together to form the now very-solid doorway.

I stared, mesmerized, as Zaffirah walked through it first, gesturing for me to follow behind her. I slowly took a step into the door of light. My eyes narrowed as they adjusted to the bright light.

A magical bounty surrounded me. The fragrant air pulled me deeper into the land. Zaffirah had disappeared, and I wasn't bothered. Not one bit. I was too absorbed by the pink-leaved trees that fanned open above me. Next to the trees, there were beds of roses in every color—mauve, lilac, white, cerise, salmon, vermillion, copper, and so many more. Where there were not any trees or roses, sunflowers, chrysanthemums, lilies, and poppies filled their spot. A butterfly with wings like the scarlet color of the amulet danced with the wind and settled daintily on the budding petals of a rose. It camouflaged into the flower completely, until I could no longer see it.

Another butterfly flew closer to me. Its wings brushed my skin and I gasped. It was not a butterfly. It landed on my hand, leaving traces of powder, but it wasn't ordinary powder. It was an iridescent, silver dust. I slowly noticed the limbs that joined to the insect's body, two arms and two legs. They were just like mine, only smaller. The creature was like one of those you read about in books, yet still different. Books could only tell you so much. To really understand something, you must see it for yourself. The length of the creature's whole body compared easily to the size of my fingernail. There were more like her, some without wings, some with pointy ears, and some with no ears at all. They peeped out from behind the trees, frightened of me.

"Welcome to Zarcane." The creature flew off my hand, leaving her magnetic voice to reverberate around me. It spoke. Like a human.

"Isra . . . Isra, my darling. Isra, come here."

It was my mother's voice. I followed the silver, chiming voice calling to me. It was almost like the voice of the tiny creature I had just held, but louder. It was her voice before she lost her mind.

I ran until I could finally see her. Tiny cherry blossoms were knotted in her hair. Her lips were turned up in a smile, and she was in a rosy dress that fanned in crinkles below the bodice line. As beautiful as the dress was, it was not the dress that complimented my mother; it was my mother that complimented the dress.

I ran toward her, and before I knew it, her delicate arms were around me. She rested her chin on the top my head, and I curled up smaller to fit her body. I felt like a four-year-old child again, being comforted by her mother after grazing her knee.

"Isra, did you see the Rose Flies? Aren't they just adorable? This place has so many interesting creatures. It's much better than our home," Zaffirah piped, skipping toward me in a tiara made of roses. She smiled at my mother, but showed no sign of surprise or excitement. I gave her a confused look, but she ignored it.

"So, did you see them? They're like beautiful little butterflies, aren't they?" Zaffirah pressed.

I nodded.

"There are so many more creatures like them. I bet you haven't seen the Crystal Creatures or the Horse Warriors.

They're called Centaurs—oh, I have so much to show you." She ended with a tinkling laugh.

"Where is this place? This Zarcane?" I addressed my mother directly, blocking my sister out.

My mother placed her hand in mine and began walking. Zaffirah wasn't far behind us. I could feel the soft, dewy grass tickle the soles of my feet. I looked down at my naked feet; I was wearing shoes before, but they were gone now.

We walked uphill for a couple of minutes before finally ending up at the mouth of a glittering cave. "*The cave of songs*," I heard a plummy voice murmur in my head.

My mother guided me inside, and my ears were instantly filled with a poignant, flute-like voice. The air had suddenly gone moist, and all I could see were tiny spots of kaleidoscopic light. I knew this place. I had been here.

"They're singing Light Worms. Stunning, aren't they?" Zaffirah mused.

My mother turned, and we were suddenly under the dim light of a sun that shined through the cracks in the ceiling where crystal stalactites were forming. She loosened her grip on my hand and took her seat on the ground next to Zaffirah. I sat down beside her. She took a deep breath before answering the questions I hadn't even had a chance to voice yet.

She started by pointing lightly at the wall behind her. I stared at the cave drawings. "It's the history of this place, God's sacred paradise. Did I ever tell you about Adam and Eve?" I shook my head, confused; the names were familiar, but I couldn't say that I had heard of them before.

"Where should I start?" Her eyes fell to Zaffirah's hand, which was currently curled around the amulet. "You'll like the story. It began the day God decided to create man. He made him from clay and breathed life into his body. He called him Adam, but Adam became lonely, so God then created him a companion, Eve. After completing his creations, he asked all the angels to bow down to the two humans. Most of the angels obeyed, but there were some that didn't. They were banished from heaven, and so they fell, losing their wings. We call them demons. Adam and Eve were then sent to a paradise—the Garden of Eden, between Heaven and Earth, home to the demons and even some angels."

She noticed my questioning look and nodded. This was the paradise God had created for the first man and woman. I was sitting on the ground where Adam and Eve would have once walked.

My mother continued: "As the story goes, God told Adam and Eve to enjoy the paradise, but not to eat the fruit of the forbidden tree of good and evil. Being humans, it didn't take much of the demons' tempting for Adam and Eve to do just that. Curiosity forced them, and as a punishment, God took away the paradise and sent them to Earth. Every human born after was not allowed to see the paradise ever again. This place has been named by our kind as Zarcane."

Zarcane . . . I knew I had been here. I was here when I used the amulet the first time. That's what Dearg called it— Zarcane. This is it.

My mother gave me a worried look. "What is it, Isra?"

"I've been here before," I murmured.

"Have you?" My mother raised her eyebrows.

"Did you know when I was here? Did you see me?" I asked.

"No, my dear, I'm sorry I did not. I didn't expect you to be here so soon," she replied, looking me in the eyes.

I nodded thoughtfully and told her to continue.

"It is said that when Adam and Eve apologized, God took mercy upon them and named them the Guardians of Zarcane. They were each given an amulet to visit this place just as they pleased. It was both a blessing and a curse. Generations have gone by, and the amulet has been passed down from mother to daughter and father to son. You are one of the Keepers of the Amulet. Just as I was."

I looked at the cave drawings. There were two circles formed in gold in the shape of the amulet. A red dye of sorts was smudged in the circles.

"As a Guardian, it is your duty to keep the borders between the Earth and Zarcane locked. Like a doorway. When the borders are unlocked, it is easier for dreamers to visit this place, and it is dangerous for a living soul. Humans who are unable to let go of their connection to Earth, and dreamers that have a habit of letting their minds wander can get stuck here. They can become lost. Their physical body dies when this happens. At the same time, creatures of Zarcane can also go to the Earth and wreak havoc. Every human life they take makes them more powerful. But there is a way to stop that. Your amulet is the key. You have to hurry, because it's already happening—"

"Stop!" I nearly yelled out. "What is Zaffirah doing here? How do I help her?"

"She's stuck. Until she has her physical body back—"

"How do I help her?"

"You can't. She must help herself."

"Isra, stop worrying about me. I'll be perfectly fine," Zaffirah chirruped.

I could have slapped her right there and then for her disregard of her own life, but I didn't for the sake of my mother. Irritated, I allowed her to continue the story. She tapped the two circles that were surrounded by the other drawings with her pink fingernails.

"These are the locks. If the two amulets are brought here in time and joined with this wall, the borders become locked. No creature or human that does not belong can pass through. That is how it's meant to be. The borders are already starting to unlock again. It is up to the next Keepers to find each other and secure the borders. You must hurry. Dreamers and demons may already be passing through. They will need you to guide them back to Earth. The creatures need Zarcane for energy. When you close the borders, those remaining on Earth will die.

"And Isra, if you need me, I'll always be right here." She took my hands in hers and placed them on my heart.

"I know you can do it. I believe in you. Use the diary. Goodbye, my sweet child." Her voice slowly got softer and when I looked up, she was fading away, her body becoming translucent.

"Wait!" I cried out in alarm. "How will I know what to do? How will I find the other Keeper?"

She answered my questions by softly pressing her lips on my forehead, and then, just like that, she was gone. In her place were several flitting creatures carried by wings of pink. The sun's light reflected off their wings in brilliant sparkles. They were the Rose Flies I had seen earlier.

I jumped up. "Zaffirah, she's gone. Where is she?"

I looked at my sister, who was still nestled peacefully on the ground. Zaffirah gave me a nonchalant look. "She had to leave. She completed her task, and now she's going." The question mark painted on my face made her sigh and continue. "Her essence belongs to God. She went back to him. She can't exactly stay here. It's not a permanent place for human souls. I think we should go now. I am so tired. Hospital beds are quite comfy, you know?"

Zaffirah pulled out the amulet that had been tucked underneath the folds of her skirt. She gave it to me. "Open the doorway," she instructed.

I did the same thing as before, kneeling and placing the amulet on the ground. Closing my eyes, I whispered the magic words. "Deala Roma Fae."

As the last syllable slipped from my tongue, the door of light appeared. Just like before. I took Zaffirah's hand and stepped forward, but she stopped me. She said, "Isra, I must stay here . . . . Until my body is healthy enough for me to be back in it, I will have to stay here."

She didn't give me a chance to react; her hands pushed me

through the doorway, and it faded away before I could look
back at her.

Nineteen

Isra

I peeked out from beneath my dark eyelashes; I was curled up on the chair beside Zaffirah's bed. My hand was still holding hers, but a cold, solid surface separated her hand from mine. I pulled out the amulet that had been trapped between our palms. The yellow rope that the amulet hung from was looped around my wrist. *Was it a dream? It couldn't have been. It felt so real.*

"Zaffirah, wake up." I nudged my sister's shoulder slightly and then waited for a response. I didn't expect her to still be in a coma. I'd seen her standing. I'd heard her talking. I had felt the pressure from her hand that was now once again limp. I didn't want to believe that she was still bed-ridden.

"Zaffirah!" My voice got louder as I squeezed her hands.

The weight of someone's hands pushed down on my shoulders. An electric current ran through them. I recognized that feeling. These hands were Ammun's.

"Isra, stop," Ammun whispered. He pulled my hands away from Zaffirah. "You're hurting her." I looked down at Zaffirah's wrists. Red rings marked them like skin-tight brace-lets. "Come on." In my dazed state, I felt his arm go around me. He guided me out of the room.

"It wasn't a dream," I murmured.

"I know," he assured, jerking me with his words.

"How do you know? *What* do you know? You don't know anything. You think I'm a fool!" I yelled angrily. I didn't know why I did. It was a build up of frustrations.

"Relax. As hard as it is for you to trust me again, I know what you saw. I'm probably one of the few that do."

"Prove it," I snapped, crossing my arms over my chest.

"I will. You saw the land between Heaven and Earth. You saw Zarcane. There were roses unlike any other, weren't there? And trees, and the Fae? Beautiful, weren't they?" He pushed his shoulders back with a smug smile.

"You're making this up," I growled

"Then I must be pretty darn good at making things up. That was exactly what you saw," he retorted, maintaining eye contact.

"How do you know all this?"

"That place was my home. I'm not exactly . . . how do I put this . . . human."

"So, what are you? Dead? Like my mother?" I scoffed, frowning.

"Try again," he muttered.

"No. You're a liar."

"Look in my eyes and tell me that." He stepped closer; I felt his hot breath on my face as his eyes bored into mine. I saw the brown mix with the shining gold flecks. The colors churned around each other.

"Look at my speed and tell me that." Before he even finished speaking, he was gone. I watched him step away from behind a medicine cart a few meters back. I remembered his strange speed. I had thought it was inhuman when I first met him.

My mouth hung open. "Contacts. Strong legs. Stop! I don't believe you! Just stop! I have enough to deal with!" I yelled.

Ammun ran back toward me. His eyes glowed with fury. For a second, I thought he was going to slap me. I squeezed my eyes shut for the impact. Nothing happened. I waited. Still nothing. I finally opened my eyes. Ammun stood before me, smiling.

"I'll make you believe me," he whispered into my ear.

He grabbed my wrist and dragged me to the rooftop of the hospital. He muttered something under his breath before placing my arms on his neck. It wasn't done forcefully. I could have pulled away if I wanted to, but I didn't. I breathed in his grassy smell and closed my eyes, comforted by his closeness.

When he was certain I wasn't going to push him away, he lifted my legs and positioned them securely on his hips. All of this he managed to do in only a few seconds.

"Ready?" he asked.

"Ready for what?"

"You'll see." He kept his grip on me.

And then, just like that, he raced from one end of the roof to the other. The ground blurred beneath me. Wind whipped my hair and lashed at my face. Then, ever so slightly, he began to rise. Up, into the air. The rooftop was no longer below us. Wings tore through his skin and protruded from his back on either side of me. They had cut through his shirt and now arched high above his head. There was no blood, or anything to suggest that they hadn't always been there.

He slowed down once we were in the air. My eyes took in every feather of his white wings. Each tip was tinged with a dark gold. They seemed so delicate. So fragile. How they could hold two whole bodies in the air was a mystery to me. I reached out to touch one, hoping my hand wouldn't tear it. The soft, velvet feathers were stronger than they looked. I felt the hard bone that lined their tops and the smooth, almost nonexistent silkiness with which they ended.

Suddenly, I shuddered as terror overcame me. Everything went white. I couldn't see. Ammun soared upward, and the endless blue sky came into view again. I bent my head to see what we had flown into, and I laughed. Below Ammun was a puffy white cloud. My damp clothes clung to me and droplets of water glistened on my skin. But it was only seconds before the cool wind dried me. Ammun landed on the rooftop of a high-rise building.

"I believe you," I said. My voice wavered ever so slightly. My certainty was shattered.

Twenty

Isra

I laid myself down on the sunbaked cement of the rooftop. Ammun had done the same. My eyes narrowed as I looked up at the blue sky above me. White wisps of clouds floated past the sun, revealing only tiny slivers of burning orange.

"I have a question," I murmured, distractedly. I held my mother's diary. In my anger, I hadn't noticed Ammun pick up my bag, but I was glad he did. I finally knew exactly how to open the diary. I was surprised it hadn't come to me earlier. The indentation in its fore edge was exactly the size of the amulet.

It was, in a sense, the keyhole, and the amulet was the key to opening it. The amulet was the master key to everything, literally and figuratively.

"Go ahead," Ammun said, looking at me expectantly.

"In the police station, how did I draw Zaffirah's kidnapper? I had never seen the man I drew. I don't even know *how* to draw. Did you do that?"

He nodded. "If you had seen that piece of paper I had in the hospital, you would've known. When you squeezed the amulet, I got this strange feeling you needed help. You might not be able to draw, but I can. I nudged your mind a little. Gave it a suggestion."

I remembered the piece of paper he had crumpled in his hands. "But how did *you* know what he looked like?"

"I didn't. I went with my instinct. I've seen a lot more on the streets than you have."

"How? You just told me you don't come from here."

"We earn our place in heaven. We're not just given one. I've lived most of my life here . . . but I don't live on the streets. I was pretending so I could be closer to you." He smiled.

"Oh," I said. That would explain his affluent look, though, to be fair, thanks to Calliel, I probably had the same look now too. "So, how do you earn it . . . your place . . . there?"

"It's simple really," he said. "I protect you."

"Why would you need to protect me?"

"You'd be surprised at how much protecting you'll need. Every Keeper has a Protector. I'm yours," he replied.

"I must be one of the lucky ones. I got you as my guardian angel," I said, laughing.

"Oh, you most definitely are." He grinned and winked at me. "But I'm probably luckier."

My neck grew hot with embarrassment at the sudden tenderness in his eyes. Ammun noticed and looked down shyly before changing the subject. "You need any help with that thing?" he asked, nudging the diary in my lap.

"No, I've got it." I pushed the amulet into the indentation. The book swallowed the amulet whole, leaving only its thread. I tried to open it, and this time, it swung open with a force much greater than my own. It was almost like it had magnified my strength.

I placed my thumb in between the flipping pages. They stopped moving. As they settled down, I looked at the page underneath my thumb. It was a diary entry written in my mother's cursive scrawl.

"Will you read it for me?" I didn't want to embarrass myself with my illiteracy, but I didn't say that to Ammun.

He nodded, took the diary form my hands, and read out loud:

Dear Diary,

I know who the other Keeper is. I found him today. I saw him in Zarcane, wandering, just as I was. After all, it is a place of so many discoveries; but you would never believe who he is. He lives so close to me. I actually know him, which is not to say I like him much. The man is not the brightest, but he is the other Keeper. I suppose we must learn to get along.

"Who was it?" I asked softly.

He shrugged. "I don't have all the answers, you know."

"Keep reading."

He peered down at the book and shook his head. "There's no more. That's the end of the entry."

Thumbing through the pages, he said, "Tell me when to stop. We'll go with your gut instinct."

Seconds passed before I told him to stop. He glanced at the page and read again:

Dear Diary,

I feel a pull to him. I don't like him, but I always want to be around him. They call it the love of Adam and Eve. It's not love, though. It's something else.

"Destiny . . ." he mumbled.

"Is she talking about my father?" I asked, turning to Ammun.

"Did she dislike your father?"

I shook my head and took the book from his hands.

"Then I doubt it." He flicked his hair off his face.

As I shut the diary, it released the amulet, and I tied it back around my neck.

Who did she dislike?

"How am I supposed to find the other Keeper if I don't even know who had the amulet before him?" I asked.

"The pull. It's like an instinct. The universe brings you to him. You don't have to do much to find him." He said it with so much conviction, I almost believed him. "Any more questions?"

"Just one." I raised myself on my elbows and stared at him curiously. "You're an angel, what else can you do?"

"I was wondering when you would ask that," he replied, smiling. "I healed you once."

"When?"

"When you were in pain . . ." He waited. I tried to remember. "You humans pay so little attention to detail, and you have terrible memory," he teased.

I glared at him.

"Relax, I was only kidding."

"I don't care," I snapped.

"Would you like me to beg for forgiveness, Royal Highness?"

I scowled at him. In return, he simply shut his eyes and ignored me. Eventually, he spoke again, oblivious to the frown that had been temporarily etched into my face.

"When my brother beat you up. That's when I healed you. Remember the *medicine*? That was my blood," he said.

I gasped and rubbed at my tongue. How could he say something like that so casually? I drank his blood! His blood!

"You're kidding. The medicine . . . it wasn't red . . ."

"Angel blood isn't red."

I stared at him for awhile, realizing he was serious. Now

that he mentioned it, I remembered the crusted slit on his wrist. It was a recent cut when I had seen it.

"What is wrong with you? That is disgusting. You gave me your blood! What were you thinking? I'm pretty sure that's basically cannibalism."

"I was thinking that you would be in excruciating pain without my blood in your system. Angel blood heals. Didn't you wonder why you had no bruises? Or broken bones?" he replied calmly.

"I was in excruciating pain anyway!"

"How long did that last again?"

I said nothing.

"That's what I thought, and I didn't appreciate the insults, by the way," he rumbled.

"Can you help my sister?" I asked suddenly. "Can you heal her like you healed me?"

He shook his head sadly. "My blood only works on the Keeper. I'm *your* protector, not hers."

"Why didn't you tell me?" I murmured, more to myself than him.

"You mean, why didn't I go, 'hey, here's a cup of my blood to make you feel better?'"

"No, I mean why didn't you tell me that you were an . . . angel?" I whispered the last word, still in awe.

"When was I supposed to tell you? When you were getting beaten up? Or when you were running away from me? Or maybe I should have told you with that devil woman in the hospital! Either way, you wouldn't have believed me until I proved it."

"Calliel is not a devil woman!"

"Are you seriously going to argue about that with *me?* I think I'd know better than you!"

"She took me into her home. She offered me food. She helped me find Zaffirah! How dare you! How dare you call her a devil woman after everything that she's done for me."

"She will do anything to get her hands on this," he said. His hand gently touched the amulet that rested in the hollow of my neck. He moved his fingers and traced the bones that protruded beneath my skin. His finger sparked and I shivered, liking his touch more than I would have cared to admit.

"She said she would help me use it better . . . that's all. I trust her," I said, unwilling to back down, desperately ignoring the motions of his hand.

He dropped his fingers from my neck. "She doesn't deserve your trust. Come on, the sun is setting. We have to get back."

I looked up at the sky. Night was pushing its way through. There was a strip of grey amongst the fiery colors of the sun. With every second that passed, the horizon grew darker.

Ammun poised himself on the edge of the building. This time, he made no attempt to help me on to his back.

"Well, my beautiful queen?" he said, smirking.

I scowled at him before getting on his back, but I felt warmth flood me at the compliment he had given.

His wings stretched out behind him and once again, he flew. He flew beside the birds that were returning to their nests. He flew below the stars that shined their light upon him. He flew with the strength and power that only an angel could have.

He landed behind the hospital. "Will you stay with her?" he asked.

"Who?"

"You know who."

"I will stay with her until I have a reason to leave. Goodnight, Ammun," I said curtly.

I started walking toward the entrance.

"Goodnight, Isra," he called out as I walked away. I felt the silent gust of air as his wings lifted him up and away.

Twenty-One

Isra

I looked up as the dark sky stole his body away from my sight. I felt my heart jump, wishing for him to return, though he had only just left. I had been too harsh with him.

"*Issssrrraaaaa.*" It had been days since the snake-like voice had whispered in my ear. I hadn't been alone for such a long time. I had almost forgotten what it sounded like. Almost. You couldn't really forget something that had tormented you for so long.

"I sssee you," it hissed. I pressed my fingers into my ears, but that didn't stop the voice. The cold fingers of fear clamped around my neck. I tried to pry them away, but they only got tighter and tighter, like a noose hanging in mid-air—my neck between the coarse rope.

"Issssrrraaaaa." I ran toward the entrance of the hospital. *"You can't hide from me, Issssraaaa."*

Someone grabbed me and lifted me into the air. I heard the sound of wings beating. Did Ammun come back? I twisted in his arms to get a look and saw Kasim holding me instead. I screamed and, realizing my mistake too late, a damp cloth was stuffed into my mouth. Gagging, the sickly, sweet stench dissolved into my system and I blacked out.

I opened my eyes, expecting Kasim, but instead, I saw trees towering high above me, their leaves fanning out like open palms worshipping the skies. I knew instantly that I was back in Zarcane. A horse-like creature galloped toward me. He was half man, half horse—a creature from another story book. Long, brown stallion legs supported his human torso. Tanned skins were tied on to his chest with thin threads of animal sinew. On his back was a quiver of arrows and a bow.

"Good evening, Keeper of Eden. You may not know me, but I am a warrior of the Abaddon. I have been sent here to alert you of her wishes. She desires an audience with you at the Red Court."

The warrior glared down at me. I met his stare, clenching my hands to stop them from shaking. His eyes shifted to the side as though he was trying to tell me something . . . a secret meant only for me. The furtive glance lasted for only a second before his cool expression was back. He was waiting for an answer, and I couldn't say no to him. His question was not a request, but a demand.

"You must come with me, Isra Kalb. It would be unwise to keep the Abaddon waiting. Take my hand. Hurry up," he commanded.

I grabbed the warrior's calloused hands. He used only his left arm to lift me onto his back. I gasped in panic as he started walking; there was nothing to hold. I felt like I was falling. My legs automatically tightened around the horse part of the creature's body. I felt only a little steadier. "How far is this Red Court?" I snapped.

"See with your eyes before you ask questions that you may learn the answers to yourself."

In the distance, there was a palace tinged with red. It had six tall towers spiraling into the sky and was surrounded by clear water. A massive tree of orange and gold, touching the clouds, sheltered the palace's gardens. Wind tugged leaves off its branches and they flew aimlessly in all directions.

"I will only say this once: no matter what you are offered to eat or drink, do not let it pass your lips. I have warned you." When we were only a few meters away, he helped me off his back and onto my own feet.

"Follow me," he instructed. He took off toward the palace at a brisk walk, and I hurried to keep up with him.

As we came closer to the palace, the low tremble of drums resounded. Guards like the centaur and other wingless creatures raised their hands in a salute. The wooden doors were opened and the portcullis behind it pulled up. Red stone parapets surrounded the turreted towers of the castle. The warrior dragged me through the royal entrance and the grass beneath my feet gradually merged into smooth, milky marble. I looked up and saw the stolen light of the stars glittering in the bulbs of crystal chandeliers. I wasn't outside anymore.

I glanced around. Everything was glowing and glittering—the walls, the curtains, the furniture. The warrior led me to an opulent hallway with golden tapestries. A chair stood at the front of the room. The back had been carved with an ancient pattern. Some of the pieces had been cut out of its back, but the plump red pillow made up for any discomfort the back of the chair may have caused.

"Welcome to the Red Court," the warrior murmured.

A resonant sound of blowing horns filled my ears, almost drowning out what the warrior said next.

"She's coming."

The song hit its last note and drifted away into the silence. The players fell to their knees, along with the warrior. I mimicked their motion. Just as I did so, the Abaddon entered. Her burgundy dress fell behind her, but it didn't drag on the floor collecting dust; it floated a few minute centimeters just above it. Her hair framed her face in loose curls that matched the color of her dress. The Abaddon met my gaze for a second, her cool, penetrating blue eyes on mine. Everything froze around me. She grinned, knowing the effect of her stare, and turned away. She was beautiful with high, protruding cheekbones and bee-stung lips.

"You may rise, Itai," the Abaddon directed the warrior.

Obediently, he rose. "Your Highness, I present the Keeper of Eden."

The previously fierce warrior now looked as tamed as a dog. He bent his head slightly, but his eyes were wide as he waited for the Abaddon's response. His expression reminded me of a child who was trying desperately to please his impossible-to-impress parents.

"I see. Thank you, Itai. You may leave now. All of you, leave us be." I looked around as the creatures dissolved into the shadows. Itai hesitated for a second, looking at me strangely, but he too eventually left. The doors slammed shut.

"Take a seat, my dear," the Abaddon instructed.

She snapped her fingers and her servants reappeared, carrying a chair for me to sit upon. I remained standing, trying desperately to ignore the temptation to bolt.

The Abaddon shrugged. "Suit yourself."

More servants entered the room. They held out flutes of golden liquid and exotic foods. One plate displayed a red fruit the size of two fists put together. It was sliced down the middle, revealing white flesh covered in tiny dark seeds. Resisting the urge to pick it up, I told myself I wasn't hungry. I wasn't living in the slums anymore. I could have food whenever I wanted.

I pulled back the hand that I had raised toward the plate and declined the offer, heeding the warning that her warrior had given me.

"So, child, you know what happens to those who eat my food?" the Abaddon asked.

Though I didn't have much of a clue as to what would actually happen if I had taken the fruit, I nodded. I wished I had asked the warrior.

"You lie," the Abaddon said. "All you know is that you shouldn't consume it. A creature of my caliber knows when it is being lied to," she continued.

I shrugged, trying to look as composed as the Abaddon herself. "Why did you call me here?" I questioned.

She ignored me and mused out loud. "That fruit would have forced you to stay in my realm, forever. If only you had tasted—"

"But I didn't."

She gave me a disapproving look for the interruption. "I am well aware of that."

"Why did you order your warrior to bring me here?" I asked again.

"I told him to bring you here because I want that charm around your neck." She held up her delicate hand as soon as she saw my mouth open. "Listen, then speak. I could give you whatever you want for that amulet. I could bring your dear little sister back—back to the reality of your world that is. Wouldn't you just adore that?"

"Why do you want it?" I asked.

"That is none of your business, Keeper. You will do as I say . . . or you will suffer. You do not know the power of the demons. You have never faced our kind before, but you will soon see that we are creatures you want on *your* side."

"And what if I don't give it you?"

"A wise question, Keeper." She smiled. "I was hoping you'd ask. Bring out the child!" she yelled to no one in particular.

A centaur dragged Zaffirah out, blindfolded, with her hands and legs bound together. She was kicking and screaming, trying to get free. It wasn't working.

"Let her go!" I screamed, running toward her. I never made it close enough. Guards appeared behind me, grabbing my arms.

"Hand over the amulet and I will," the Abaddon snarled.

Vomit worked its way up my throat at the thought of parting with the amulet. I struggled, trying to get free, but I couldn't. I could hardly move without wrenching my arms off my shoulders. The guards had an iron grip. I would have purple bruises by tomorrow in the places where their hands had touched my skin.

"If you won't willingly cooperate, my dear Keeper, I will simply have to make you," the Abaddon lilted, rising from her throne.

I had to get out of here before she touched me. I had to get back to my body before she took the amulet. I had to go. I glanced at Zaffirah, still kicking and screaming. She was yelling my name and yet again, I was going to abandon her. I shut my eyes, holding back my tears. My sister would have to wait.

"Deala Roma Fae," I whispered, knowing I had no other choice. The Abaddon's eyes widened in surprise and the guards tightened their grip on my arms, but it was no use. Ribbons of white light wrapped themselves around my body and the world faded from my sight.

My eyes flew open. The strong scent of tobacco instantly met my nose. It went down my throat and aroused uncontrollable fits of coughing. I coughed until I had no energy left to cough any more. I gulped in what little oxygen there was in the air around me, my throat prickling. Each breath of the pungent scent tangled a knot in my stomach.

The cloudy wisps of grey smoke danced around the room. My eyes came to focus on a boy, perched lazily on the edge of a table on the other side of the room. I tried to walk toward him and, unable to do so, I noticed the rope coiled around my ankles. That same rope was around my wrists too. My sister was trapped back in that world, and here I was, trapped in ours.

"Who are you?" I yelled at the boy. "Let me go. Get this off me!"

The boy looked up. In his hand was the source of the smoke. He lifted a cigarette out of the packet. Holding it carefully between his forefinger and thumb, he lit it with a single flicker from his lighter. The boy brought the cigarette to his lips and sucked in. I watched him walk toward me, the smoke parting around him. He came closer, but it was only when he stood meters away that I recognized his broken nose and jagged scar. It was Ammun's brother. A spasm of anger and fear rippled through me. I tried to stand so I could meet him eye to eye, but I couldn't move.

"I'm not the helping kind. *Maaf kar do, guriya.* Maybe, my brother will come to your service?"

I looked away from him. I looked at the creamy, stained wallpaper. He put his burning hand under my chin and turned my face up toward him. His sharp nails drew beads of blood from my neck. Its warmth trickled down my throat.

"Look at me when I talk to you!" he growled.

I spat in his eye and jerked out of his grasp. He swiped the spittle away.

"Do that again, and I'll make sure you regret it," he warned.

I heard a scuffle of shoes behind me. There was someone else standing there. He cleared his throat. I followed his gaze to the other boy. A green-eyed boy. Someone I knew oh so well. Even with the smoke distorting him, I knew it was Farid. He avoided my stare, and when he spoke, his voice shook like a baby's rattle.

"Kasim *bhai,* you said you wouldn't hurt her."

"No, Farid, I said I wouldn't *kill* her," Kasim replied. His voice was patronizing, yet masked with a fake sweetness. The sound of a snake charmer's flute. I watched Farid's mouth open in shock. I could see him contemplating whether to go against Kasim or not. He chose the latter and silently nodded.

"Next time, do remember what I tell you, and never ever challenge me," Kasim snapped. "Are we clear?"

Farid's head bobbed up and down quickly. "Sorry, Kasim *bhai*."

I stared at him unbelievingly. What was Farid doing here? What was he doing with Kasim? Why was he calling him brother?

Kasim waved away the apology. "Just don't let it happen again. Now, I have to go find my dear sweet brother. I'll be gone for a while. You can prove your worth. Don't let the girl out of your sight, understand?"

"I understand. You can trust me."

"Good, because if I find her gone . . ." He looked up, giving Farid a crooked smile. Then he winked, dropped his cigarette butt, crushed the glowing red embers, and walked out of the room. His message was clear.

I glanced up at Farid; his eyes were on the door, following Kasim as he left.

"How do you know him?" I asked finally.

"He saved me."

"Why? From what?"

"It doesn't matter." He paused, opened his mouth, and then closed it again.

"Say whatever it is you want you say," I muttered.

He stared at me for awhile. "Remember how your father built my family a house?" he asked finally.

"Yes, I remember. What has this got to do with your *friend* tying me up and bringing me here?"

"I just want you to listen. Your father's reasons weren't as selfless as you think. My mother was your father's mistress a long time ago—"

"I don't want to hear whatever lies Kasim has fed to your thick brain," I snarled.

"They're not lies. Please, listen."

"Fine, but don't ask me to believe you too."

"Believing is your choice, but I know it's the truth! Kasim brought me home after he saved me. My mother was yelling, and my father was just standing there, listening to her yell. He wouldn't say anything! She hit him. She yelled for your father. I heard everything. When your father wanted to end the affair many years ago, he was too late. She was pregnant with his child, and she wanted to leave my pathetic fisherman father for yours. She thought your father loved her. Boy, was she wrong. She threatened him, telling him that she would tell your mother everything that had transpired between them. So your father bribed her with the promise of a new house . . . food. Even when sometimes your family starved without a single meal, we got ours . . . at least, some of us did."

I took it in slowly. At first, I was fuming that Farid would dare to make such an accusation. I stared at him, looking for signs that everything he was telling me was a lie. The flaring of his nose; the rapid blinking of his eyelids. I knew when Farid was lying. Those were his telltale signs, but right now, there was nothing—not a single sign to tell me he was lying. But I knew he had to be. My father was a good man. He would never have done that to my mother. He would never have done that to *us*. I couldn't believe it. I didn't want to believe it, but . . . the puzzle pieces fit, I realized. I had seen the two talking in private in the corners of her tiny house on more than one occasion.

"Does that mean? Are you my . . . ?"

He shook his head. "My older brother. Asad. He's your father's son. He's your half brother." He looked at the ground, shuffling his feet.

"I thought I was just unlucky, born into a broken family. But it wasn't broken from the start! Your father came, and he hammered and hammered and turned my family into jagged pieces of glass that will never fit together again!" His eyes glistened. Instantly, he wiped away the moisture.

I wanted to comfort him. I tried. "It's okay . . ." My voice cracked. "It'll get better." Though, I honestly didn't know if it would. I hadn't realized that Farid had been so neglected. I had always thought he was close to his father. I hadn't realized how torn his family was and there was no one to blame for it but my very own father. "It's okay . . . I know what you're feeling," I said softly.

"Stop it! I don't need your pity!" he retorted. "I'll get something much better with that." He gestured to my neck. My bound hands instinctively touched the amulet resting at the base of my neck.

My lips curled above my teeth, but I calmed myself down before I could say anything I knew I would later regret. "What do you want with my amulet?" I asked, slowly.

"I have the other one," he said softly.

I gasped. Of all people, Farid Hassan, my temperamental friend, was the other Keeper; but another part of me realized that, of course, he was the other Keeper. He was always in every place that I happened to be. There might as well have been a giant sign from the universe pointing to him saying *this is the guy you're looking for*. "Do you know what that means?" I asked.

He nodded. I wasn't done. I had to be sure. "How could you not see Dearg? If you are truly the other Keeper, you would have the sight."

"Dearg?"

"That day when you beat up the boy and followed me. You asked me who I was talking to. I said no one. I lied."

"I saw the creature, but I thought I was imagining it. I didn't believe it. I blinked, and I couldn't see him anymore. I don't know why. I guess the Keeper blood is stronger in you than it is in me."

Thrrruuuummm. My ears pricked instantly, trained to the buzzing hum. I knew that noise. It was the noise of the amulet. Not my own, but the *other* amulet. I looked at Farid, but he hadn't heard anything . . . at least, not yet. It was getting louder, just like my own. It was coming from the room beside this one. As the sound grew, my amulet got warmer, pulsing with power.

"Farid . . ." I said carefully. "Where is the amulet now?"

He shrugged. "I gave it to Kasim. He wanted it. He saved me," he repeated.

"Kasim wanting the amulet didn't strike you as strange at all?"

He shook his head.

I would have to spell it out for him. "Okay, let's try this again. Did him tying me up seem strange to you?"

He hesitated this time before shaking his head.

"Farid, listen to me. He's not a good guy. I am willing to bet he's working with the Abaddon. She took my sister! Get your amulet, untie me, and get us out of here before it's too late."

"I can't."

I scowled at him, and then I realized. He had no idea where the amulet was.

"Farid, I know where it is. Untie me. I'll get it." For a split second, I saw relief in his face, but it was quick to disappear. Quick to evaporate into thin air.

"I don't believe you. I trust Kasim," he said softly, more to convince himself than me.

"Untie me. I'll show you," I pleaded. "What happened to *our* trust?"

He glared at me, fuming with anger. "I can't untie you, Isra," he yelled. "I trust Kasim. He's going to help me," he mumbled.

He had never yelled at me like that before. Others maybe, but with me, he had always been able to control his fury. "So that's it then, you'll do whatever he says?" I asked. He didn't even need to nod. I knew his answer.

"He's not going to hurt you. He needs us both for our plan to work," he said with conviction. "Just this once, I need *you* to trust *me*."

"How can I trust you if *you* don't trust *me*?" I asked. "I know where the amulet is. Please just let me show you." I held on to the hope that if Farid could just hold the amulet in his hands, he would know that he was being played by Kasim.

His shoulders sagged as he argued with himself over what to do. His eyebrows were furrowed over his narrowed eyes, making his conflicted emotions blatant on his face. He was an open book that didn't want to be read. I knew him well enough to know that he wanted the amulet, but he wasn't going to admit it.

"No. You want to escape. I know it. If I let you go and you run, you'll ruin everything. We have a plan. I can't let you just go." Something about the way he said *plan* made me worry about what he was thinking. It didn't seem like a plan that involved saving the world. He was filled with too much hatred for my father and his mother to care for saving anyone at that moment.

"You are an idiot!" I pursed my lips.

"Shut up! I don't want to hear you anymore."

He walked away from me. Minutes passed before I ultimately broke the silence. "I need the toilet."

He yanked me up by my wrists and quickly let go when I was on my feet, as though my skin had burnt him. "This better not be your escape plan. Don't try anything stupid. I'm faster than you. I'm stronger than you," he reminded.

I didn't need to be reminded. One look at him and I knew for sure, I would lose in a physical fight if it came to that. I shuffled slowly behind him. This time, I didn't even attempt to talk to him. I knew it was useless. I *was* thinking of escaping. Escaping in such a way that I wouldn't be caught. Escaping with *his* amulet. He wouldn't be doing any good with it anyway, from what I could tell.

"Can you walk any slower?" he growled after a few seconds.

"Why don't you tie your feet up too and we'll race, see who's faster then," I retorted.

He scowled in return. "Go. Hurry up!" He pointed at the door, pushed me through, and banged the door shut in my face.

I poked my head back out and held out my tied hands. "Little help, please?"

He grunted, hesitating at first, but deciding I would be just as harmless with my hands free as I was now. He pulled out a pocket knife and cut away the rope.

"Go," he snapped.

I went back inside the bathroom. My right hand touched the knob, and my left hand fiddled with the lock. *Click. Click.* Now, he couldn't come in. And I couldn't come out. I was safe for now . . . but trapped. I twisted the tap and let it drip into the basin while looking for an exit. There were no windows. Seconds passed. The flow of water from the tap slowed. It was barely louder than a whisper now.

"How long does it take to go to the toilet?" he called.

"Quite long if you're looking for a magical amulet," I muttered to myself.

Thrrruuuuuummmm. The other amulet. I could hear it getting louder. I turned left and right, throwing open cupboards. Shampoo. Soap. Razor. Shaving cream. Tooth paste. Brush. Everything but the other amulet. Farid hammered at the door with his fists. "Isra! Get out!"

He was using his legs now, kicking the door. With every blow, I watched its rusted hinges shudder. They were getting weaker. And then suddenly, there was nothing. Silence. I heard a voice.

"Farid, what in the world are you doing?" Kasim asked skeptically. He was back.

"Owwww," I mumbled. There was a burning around my neck. The amulet was no longer simply warm. It was hot. Burning hot. I untied the yellow thread from around my neck—careful not to touch the amulet itself. It whizzed away out of my hand, as soon as it was off, stopping at the foot of the tub. My palm rested on the tile the amulet was on while I looked inside the tub itself. As I pressed my weight on the tile, it moved under my hand. I pushed it harder, and this time, it came away completely.

I peeked through the opening. Black. It was all black. Nothing but darkness. *Thrumm.* I looked again, and this time, I saw it. It was emitting its own red light. My fingers extended to curve around its solid exterior. I had it.

"You what? Are you telling me she's in there? Get her out! Now!" Kasim yelled.

It only took me a moment to realize what I had to do next.

"Deala Roma Fae!" I shouted the words, and they didn't fail me.

"Stop!" he roared, but I ignored him, concentrating on the door of light.

Boom. The kicking had finally broken the hinges. If only it had held up for a few moments longer . . . . I glanced at Kasim and Farid for a little less then a second before stepping into Zarcane, but as I did so, the other amulet rocketed out of my hand. Kasim ran in after me, leaving it behind.

Twenty-Two

Farid

"Friends come and go," I whispered to myself. *Friends come and go. Friends come and go. Friends come and go.* This became a chant in my head as Kasim yelled at me. I didn't hear anything. All I could think about was Isra.

I had known Isra my whole life. She was the only friend that I hadn't hurt. I thought I never would, because there was something about her that made me care. Hell, she was the only one I could even call my friend. Everyone else simply hated me, and I couldn't help hating them. I tried to hate her when I found out. I tried to hate her because of everything her father did . . . but I couldn't.

Isra reminded me of Maya, and in any other situation, I would have been the one to save her, not hurt her. But I needed the amulet. I needed to get it back. I needed to do what was right—for my father and everything that he was cheated out of . . . his wife, his family, his home. And the rest of the world was no better.

My father was a living example of all the pain in this world. He embodied it. He lived through it, and only because some man was not kind enough to stay away from his wife. Isra's father tore our family apart. He was supposed to be a good human being, but he was far from it. Now, it was my turn. I would tear our world apart, just like he did my family.

Kasim backed up and gestured with a scowl for me to get out of his way. Before I even had the chance to move, he rammed into the door with his shoulder jutting out. The door shook from the impact, but remained otherwise in place. As soon as he saw that the door wasn't about to crash open at his touch, he kicked it, backed up again, and ran straight into it. The door wasn't as strong as it looked. This time, it splintered off its hinges with a crack.

A blinding light flashed into my eyes. For a second, I couldn't see anything but white. My eyes adjusted. Everything afterward happened almost in slow motion—a suspension in time. Kasim moved like he was underwater. He lunged for Isra, his arms outstretched to suffocate her in his grasp. She moved into the white light. A blur of red ricocheted out of her hand and into mine as she stepped out of this realm and into the next. In that second, I watched her reach for it, reconsider, and allow the white light to completely conceal her from my sight. I recognized that light. I had seen it once before, when my father had led me to a strange land in a dream I'd had not so long ago. I knew exactly where it would lead her. Kasim ran in after her.

My body fell to the ground as I clutched the amulet between my fingers. I lost her for this. I rocked it back and forth between my palms. Was it worth it?

"You. Open the doorway. *Now!*"

I turned around. Standing before me, with wings arched above his head, was another angel. "What are you waiting for?" he growled.

He snatched the amulet from my hands and yanked me to my feet. "Open the doorway, or I won't hesitate to *make* you do it," he warned. His fists were clenched at his sides, emphasizing his words as he crouched down to face me. His eyes glared, daring me to argue—daring me to make a move. His irises were so dilated that I almost thought I saw the coppery colors in them move.

I took the amulet from him and muttered the words I had heard Isra say. I didn't know what else to do. I wasn't sure that they would work. It was the first time I was trying to open the doorway on my own, awake. I had only seen Zarcane in my dreams, and my dreams hadn't required the amulet. I made a silent prayer and opened my mouth. "Deala Roma Fae."

There was a flash of light that instantly disappeared. It didn't stay long enough for us to pass through. I looked up at him, pathetically.

"Louder!" he snarled.

I tried again, this time yelling the words, hoping for my sake that they would work.

"*Deala Roma Fae!*"

The door emerged with a burst of light and remained, awaiting our entry.

The angel glanced at it. His face softened instantly as relief flooded through his body. He hadn't had any confidence that I could make the doorway appear. Forgetting my fear of the creature, I took pleasure in my feat and gave him a smug smirk. He ignored it, and then, without warning, he grabbed me by the cuff of my shirt, snatched the amulet from where I had placed it on the ground, and rushed through the doorway without a moment's hesitation.

Twenty-Three

Isra

"Hello, Isra," Kasim growled. His voice was like ice, cold and hard, piercing my thoughts.

I looked at his eyes. Cobalt flames glowed menacingly in his irises. He was angry. Angrier than angry. He was furious. I wanted to run, as fast as I could . . . but I knew there was no point. He would catch me. He was more powerful here. His power was overflowing, immense. It wasn't human. The energy that radiated from his body made him seem as though he had wings made of incorporeal coils of white. It looked as though his fractured soul had been captured fleeing from his body. The feathers lined across his wing bones were a fine, blackish silver.

"Scared? Good. You should be."

I squeezed my ears with the palms of my hands. His voice was painful. I cowered on the ground. As defenseless as the ants that I had crushed underneath me.

"Kasim! Your damsel in distress needs you!"

I turned at the voice. Ammun! His wings extended to their full length, towering meters above him, uncontrollably manic, thrashing the wind. Ammun had one arm around Farid's neck, choking him. Farid's head was bowed in defeat. In Ammun's other hand was the amulet. The one I had left behind. Farid's amulet.

"So does yours!" Kasim responded. He ran with the inhuman, lightning speed that I could only expect from a creature with wings. It took me a moment before I realized he was running toward me.

"You touch her, and the boy dies," Ammun said calmly, as if he expected his brother to say just that.

"You wouldn't! You wouldn't hurt a fly, brother!" Kasim taunted, as though he wanted Farid to be hurt. Knowing him, he probably didn't care much who got hurt.

"Would you risk it? If he dies, you die," Ammun replied. Kasim shrugged him off, but made no further move toward me. I wondered what Ammun meant when he said "*if he dies, you die*," but I knew now was not exactly the right time to ask. Kasim turned on Farid.

"You stupid boy! You opened the portal for him!" Kasim waved his arms around, his eyes retaining their menace.

"Your brother—he forced me. I couldn't help it," Farid gasped out. He raised his head and looked at me with his sad, verdant eyes. I pitied him.

"Brother, don't you see? The Abaddon can help us. We can have a home. A home where we won't have to deal with these humans, or care for them, or protect them! *He* won't be able stop us! He won't be able to make us do his work for him! Don't you see that we will be free, and those humans and their filthy planet will be destroyed."

Kasim's eyes glazed over with longing. That look made me wonder if the *He* that Kasim was talking about was God. It would have made sense. God had told his angels to bow down to his human creations. He was an angel, wasn't he? An angel tired of bowing to the humans.

Ammun landed lightly on the ground in front of Kasim. "It was never my decision. My job, *our* job, is to protect the Keepers so they can make that decision. It is up to them whether the human race lives or dies. And your life is connected with his—the Keeper. You will protect him, or die trying." Ammun spoke slowly, pronouncing each and every single one of his syllables with care.

"Brother, we can influence their decisions. Look." Kasim pointed at Farid. Ammun still had him in a headlock. I watched him flinch and let Farid go. Farid stepped away from him quickly and glared at Kasim, but said nothing.

"Fine. I have no mercy for you. If you are not on my side,

then you will die, protecting her." Kasim echoed Ammun's words. He spoke out for the final time and then burst into a ball of flames. Wings and all. He was on fire.

He aimed a roundhouse kick at Ammun's gut. Unperturbed, Ammun took the kick like it was nothing. Any human would have crumpled on the ground, gagging, but Ammun just bent his knees and brought his arms up. He was poised for a fight.

"Stop!" I yelled. Ammun didn't even turn to look at me. His eyes were on Kasim, and Kasim's were on him.

"Farid, hold her back!" Without a glance at Farid, or me, Kasim spoke the words with a steely serenity, and Farid came toward me with the obedience of a robot.

"Don't you dare," I snarled.

He ignored my words and put his arms around me in a strange embrace. I felt his muscles tighten. He was holding me back.

"My father wants this," he mumbled.

"Do you honestly believe that?" I snapped.

"Yes. I'm getting revenge for all the pain and hurt that your father made him live through," he replied mechanically.

I gaped at him with my mouth wide. The Farid I knew had hurt many, but he had never been a killer. I would never have imagined him intentionally wanting to take someone's life . . . until now. And it was not just *a* life that he wanted to take, but *millions*.

He needed my amulet for that. He was planning on destroying the amulets and every life on Earth along with it. With the amulets destroyed, the borders would be gone, and Earth would be infested with demons. He never intended to save me because he cared. He needed me for his plan to work, and with Kasim's support, he was convinced it was going to work. He was an ignorant fool.

"You have no right to destroy our world because of what you believe your father secretly wants! Damn it! My father made a mistake. It will torture him in his afterlife. But you are about to make an even bigger mistake," I shrieked.

Kasim lunged again. Another punch. Another kick. Ammun blocked them all. Panting, Kasim stepped back and wiped the sweat off his forehead. *Thwaaackkk*. Ammun's fist crashed into Kasim's nose. I heard the bone break and watched as his glittering, ocher blood trickled down his chin. He glowered at Ammun with a wrath so potent he looked as though a furious storm was raging inside him. Ammun stepped back as Kasim sprang on the balls of his feet, aiming with his fists, throwing more punches. Ammun extended his wings and shot up in to the sky. Kasim jetted off at his heel.

"That doesn't matter. Our world is a sad, cruel place. No life is innocent. Humans don't deserve to live," Farid said monotonously, as though he was repeating a fact he had committed to memory. "My father could not destroy our world, because it takes *two* Keepers to save millions, and *two* to destroy them."

"You're wrong. If your father had wanted to destroy the borders, he would never have locked them. You would never have lived to receive the amulet. You can't misuse the power you have been given!"

"It is not misuse. It is better use, and now, I need you to give me your amulet."

"You really think I will help you?" I raised my eyebrows in incredulity. Not only was he intent on destroying every human life, but he expected my help to do it.

"I thought you would understand," he said softly.

"Understand what? You know me well enough to know that I would never have joined you in your killing spree! Farid, you are insane," I spat the words in disgust. "I was wrong to think that there was any goodness in you."

"Your opinion means nothing to me." His voice wavered slightly, and I found myself believing otherwise.

"Fine, forget about me. But what about Maya? Remember her? What you want to do with the amulets will kill her along with everyone else."

Farid hesitated, and his fingers loosened their grip on me. "She might already dead," he mumbled. I remembered seeing Maya in my dreams, but for all I knew, the girl could be like Zaffirah, waiting for her body to heal so she could go back to it. There was still hope.

"I saw her here," I said, hardly moving my eyes from watching Kasim and Ammun fight.

There were more kicks. More punches. And then they were falling. My hands squeezed with fear. Fear for Ammun. His back hit the ground with Kasim on top of him. Arms and legs entangled, Kasim's fists sank into Ammun's stomach. They were even, both their faces coated in the thick, glittering bronze liquid that was angel blood. Kasim rose off Ammun and wobbled on his feet. He backed away, catching his breath for round two. I had to help Ammun, or this fight would continue for hours. Neither of them could beat each other, but they could die trying.

"You did?" he asked. I could hear the panic in his voice. *Good, let him worry*. I was in no mood to comfort him.

"Farid, let me go! *Now*!" I yelled.

"I can't." His answer came instantly. It was automatic.

His arms didn't loosen further, but they didn't tighten around me either. I kicked him with everything I had. I didn't expect to hurt him, but he did. His arms let go for a second, and that second was enough. I closed my eyes and ran, reaching for Ammun while picturing the cave of songs in my head. I was so desperate that I found myself hoping the amulet would magically transport both of us to the safe haven of the cave. "Deala Roma Fae," I whispered quickly and the white light blinded both of us.

When I opened my eyes that was exactly where we were—safe, for the moment.

Ammun was bent over, on one knee. I lifted his head to see if he was okay. His skin was stained amber everywhere. He gave me a pained look, but as I stared into his eyes, straight into the depth of his soul, I felt affection so deep, my breath stopped in my chest. I looked away, and the moment was gone.

I ripped a piece of my shirt and dabbed it at Ammun's injuries, the ones not on his face, to give me a distraction. He took it from my hand and murmured a thank you.

Twenty-Four

Farid

I don't know how it happened exactly; whether I intentionally let her go or if, in a moment of contemplation, she identified my weakness, kicked me, and escaped. Either way, it was a strange relief that she was gone. I understood the angel's fury now. His life depended on Isra staying alive. He had no choice. He *had* to protect her, and she would therefore be as safe as she could be with him at her side. That thought calmed me.

"Idiot. Have you no strength at all? You couldn't even hold back that pitiful waif of a girl!" Kasim snorted. His eyes blazed as he glared down his nose at me. "You're pathetic," he spat out.

"Damn you, Kasim," I muttered.

"What did you say?" he scoffed.

I took a deep breath. "I said *damn you!*" I barked. He flinched, not at all expecting my outburst. I took pleasure in his momentary discomfort. He looked like he was about to hit me, but he didn't.

"You need me as much as I need you," he said, carefully, regaining his composure.

"That's where you're wrong. Your life ends with mine." I grinned manically.

Kasim let out a throaty laugh at that statement. "What are you going to do? Kill yourself?" he sneered. I hadn't meant the words I said. They were intended as a threat to scare him. But seeing his reaction made me realize it was the only thing I held over him.

Kasim mistook my silence as submission and spoke again. "That's what I thought," he snickered.

Twenty-Five

Isra

"What did you mean when you said '*if he dies, you die?*'"

"As guardian angels, our lives are connected with yours. We must live to protect you, and die protecting you. If we fail, we die. Sometimes, others replace us . . . that is, if the Keeper is still alive. When the Keeper dies, it is our fault, and death is our punishment." Ammun said this matter-of-factly, devoid of any emotion.

"Don't you get a say?" I asked.

"We were made to serve without question. Those who questioned—those who went against *him*—chose the side of the demons. You know, so far it hasn't been particularly difficult to protect you, despite your constant rendezvous with danger," he teased.

"I don't go looking for it, Ammun," I snapped.

"You walk around so vulnerable and naïve. It would be strange if you didn't get into trouble." He paused and gave a defeated sigh. He was fiddling with his bracelet again, avoiding my gaze. "It's . . . frustrating. I wish you could protect yourself better."

"I'm sorry you got stuck with the *foolish* Keeper," I muttered, and I was genuinely apologetic.

"I didn't mean that . . . . You don't get it, Isra," he replied.

"Then what did you mean, Ammun?" I asked.

"I hate seeing you hurt. I hate seeing you in trouble. It hurts me when you're in pain. Isra, I care for you. I care for you in a way I'm not supposed to," he murmured softly. I had to strain to hear him, but when I did my heart thumped, dancing to some melodious, joyful tune that my ears couldn't hear.

His eyes took me in. He was analyzing every blink and twitch that came across the features of my face. He was trying to understand my emotions. The gold flecks circled around his irises as he leaned closer, almost unaware of his slight movement. I could feel the warmth of his breath brush across my upper lip . . . and his smell. It was the smell of the sun warming the earth after a storm.

"You're beautiful, stubborn, strong, and full of life," he whispered.

He raised his hand, and it stayed suspended in mid-air for a few seconds before he cupped my cheek. His fingers raised the tiny hairs at the back of my neck. It was an electric touch, as light as a feather. My head tilted ever so slightly upward, and our eyes locked. There were but a few centimeters between us—a few insignificant centimeters.

He waited. I waited. We both waited, for what? I wasn't entirely sure, but one thing I knew for certain was that he wanted this. I could tell by the look in his eyes, and all I wanted was to kiss him back. I leaned in closer, and he finally gave into the desire. He pressed his lips on mine, parting them tenderly. The strangely gentle strength of his kiss enveloped me. It gained in momentum and suddenly, I was wrapped around his body. In that second, I tasted the possibility of forever.

Then, just as swiftly as he had kissed me, he pulled away. He went as far as he could from me and only mumbled two words in place of an explanation: "I'm sorry." He opened his mouth as though he intended to say more, but shut it again, at a loss for words.

"Why? Is it because I'm not . . . like you?" I asked softly.

He sighed, and I knew I was right. I didn't want to hear him confirm my words. I wouldn't be able to bear it. I wanted to stop them, but they came anyway. The inevitable truth.

"I wish it didn't have to be like this. Dammit, Isra. I'm an angel. My kind can't get married to humans. We don't even physically feel like you do. We can't live away from our duties. We have only one love, and that is God. *Only* God.

I'm sorry. I shouldn't have . . ." He broke off and turned away from me. It was almost like he was trying to convince himself rather than me. He couldn't even bear to look at me anymore. I had destroyed him by returning his kiss, and there was nothing I could do to put all his pieces back together again.

"What do you mean you don't physically feel? Are you saying you didn't feel anything when you kissed me?"

"I felt it, but I felt it in here." His palm covered his chest in the place where I imagined his heart. "I can't *physically* feel you."

"So, what are you saying? You can only be with another angel? Is that it? Your kind has children! You have a brother. You must have a mother. That's only possible through physical feelings."

"No, that's not how it works . . . not for us, at least. We're made of fire, and just like God did with humans, he blew life into us angels. He used the same breath for my brother and me. So we're connected—as siblings, but there was no birth or marriage or any other romantic love. God is both my mother and father."

"It's not fair," I said after awhile. "So, that's it then, fire can't mix with mud."

"You don't understand. I chose this life. I chose to give my heart and soul to him."

"How can you choose to be an angel?" I snapped.

"I have to go," he mumbled, unwilling to answer. I suppose I hadn't really expected him to answer. What was done was done. Now, all he could do was regret, and it was my fault. I should have pulled away when I had the chance. I should have, but I knew that nothing in the world would have made me want to, and in that moment, I knew that he had wanted it too. I knew he had. He must have.

Twenty-Six

Farid

"**R**emember to bow. The Abaddon is very fond of her respect."

I nodded, saying nothing.

"And try not to stare."

I nodded again.

"And when she speaks to you, refer to her as Your Highness."

"I understand, Kasim," I muttered, gritting my teeth.

The brassy sound of horns drifted through the room, and the strange creatures around us went down on one knee. Kasim yanked me to the ground with him. I cursed him under my breath as pain blossomed in my knees upon hitting the hard marble.

I glanced up as the Abaddon entered the room. Her hair was the color of an overripe plum and as wild and untamed as burning flames. I couldn't help but notice the smooth curve of her breasts peeking from her low-cut dress. She was more lovely than any person I had ever seen.

"Rise, my dear Kasim! Oh, how nice it is to see you again. It's been a long time," she sang out, giving a girlish laugh.

Kasim rose to meet her. She took his coarse hands in hers and smiled. They made quite a pair. Kasim, rough and bloodied from the fight with his brother, and the Abaddon, beautiful and almost delicate.

"What brings you here? I see you have brought a friend," she said, giving me a cursory glance before returning her blue eyes to Kasim.

"I wish I could say that I have come simply to gaze upon your beauty once more, Your Highness, but I have brought news of the amulets and a proposition."

"I see. We shall speak in private then. Syerra, please show them into our *humble* abode," she instructed, clapping her hands in joy. "I'll be with you shortly," she said.

A young woman with skin the color of grass one second and the blue of the sky the next came forward. With every movement she made, her skin glowed with a new color. I wasn't certain I even had names for some of the colors her skin turned.

"If it pleases you, Your Highness," she said, bowing. Her skin flushed purple. I couldn't pull my eyes away from her. "Follow me," she said, turning to us.

The strange woman walked us through the brightly lit corridors. Portraits of the Abaddon decorated the walls in golden frames. The paintings bore little similarity to the Abaddon's true beauty. I noticed there was no one else in any of these pictures, just the Abaddon herself.

Syerra opened the doors to a room with a fireplace. The flames danced over the crackling wood. She gestured for us to enter. Plush sofas and armchairs nestled on a geometrically woven carpet of dull creams and browns.

"My mistress will be with you soon," Syerra said quietly, turning to leave.

Before she could, Kasim approached her with a cruel grin. He snaked his arm around her small waist. Her skin turned dark in shock. It was almost black. "Don't go just yet, beautiful. We'll be needing some entertainment while we're waiting," he teased.

She pulled at his arms, but he didn't remove them. "B-b-but h-h-how can I entertain you?" she whimpered.

"Oh, just a little bit of this." He looked intently at Syerra. Her eyes opened wide in panic as her hips moved sensuously, dancing to a song we couldn't hear. They moved without her control.

"What are you doing to her?" I asked urgently.

"Teaching her how to entertain us," he replied, without taking his eyes off the woman.

She was tugging at her shirt now, pulling it over her head. Kasim took in her naked shape with hungry eyes.

"Stop it," I said, disgusted.

"You don't like the show? Maybe she should get rid of her skirt too."

Right on cue, her thumbs went under the waistband of her skirt. Her face was begging him to stop. She opened her mouth, trying to say something, but no words would come out.

The door creaked opened and Kasim finally looked away from the poor woman. She grabbed her shirt and covered herself, moving as far away as she could from Kasim.

The Abaddon glided into the room, taking in the scene. Her eyes narrowed as she looked from Syerra to Kasim. "Leave us," she said finally to Syerra.

"Yes, Your Highness," she mumbled, bowing, before running out of the room.

"Why must you torture my servants so?" the Abaddon questioned. I was surprised to hear that her voice held no anger. I would have slapped Kasim's head right off his neck if I had the power I knew she surely had. He was my protector, sure, but only now did I realize how far he truly was from a good person.

"We all need our playthings, do we not?" Kasim replied, smirking.

"Yes, I suppose we do," she said with a sigh. "Now, tell me, what is this proposition you speak of?"

Twenty-Seven

Isra

I paced restlessly, unable to stop myself. I had talk to Ammun, but I wasn't sure how to start the conversation, and the endless pounding in my chest was not helping. I finally approached Ammun like one would approach a skittish deer.

"We have to focus. Forget what just happened if you must, but please help me do what I need to. That's your job, isn't it? As soon as I close the borders, you will never have to see me again. Do you have the other amulet?" I asked, careful to mask the hurt in my tone.

I saw the light fade from his eyes. The brightness that I'd drowned in when I kissed him was gone because I had sucked it out of him. It was my fault. I had drained it from his body. I shook my head, trying to shut my mind up.

"Well?" I asked.

He felt around in his pockets. Patting them. Poking them. He was so sure that he had the amulet. I shouldn't have been surprised. Somehow, the amulet always managed to go back to the Keeper.

"Kasim . . . he must have grabbed it," he muttered.

"We have to get it back," I replied instantly, tactfully avoiding his gaze. Focusing on the issue of the missing amulet was a welcome distraction from everything I was feeling for Ammun.

"I know. I'll get it . . . alone," he answered.

My shoulders almost sagged with relief, but it only took me a moment to realize I couldn't let him do this alone. My sister was there. I had to help her. "No, I'm coming with you," I said.

"No, you're not," he retorted. His voice had a forceful quality that left no more room for arguing. "It's safest for you to stay here," he said, softening his tone.

"My sister is there. I can't—"

"*Shh*. Be quiet for a second. I hear something," he said. He got up and ran to the entrance of cave. He listened for another second before going outside. He came back with a giant boulder and placed it over the mouth of the cave.

I would never get used to how easily speed and strength came to him.

"What are you doing?" I asked.

He hushed me instantly. His body was tense. I kept my eyes on him and my ears strained to hear what he heard. And then, I finally heard it. Hooves. The pounding of hooves each time they touched the ground.

Crashh.

It was Itai. He broke open the makeshift rock door that Ammun had placed to block the entrance, transformed it into dust with his fist. Silver particles flew toward us. In one single, agile movement, Ammun whipped out the knife he had stored in his shoe. It was like the one he had given me. A twin.

"Go, run," Ammun whispered into my ear.

I shook my head in bewilderment. "I'm not going anywhere. We're in this together."

I held out my palm for him to hold. Hoping he would . . . but almost certain that he wouldn't. The thought of grasping my hand was too repulsive to bear. He couldn't even look at me. I was about to let my hand fall when Ammun tangled my fingers into his. Warm stings pulsed between our skins. The electricity I'd felt emanating from him since the first time he'd touched me was back and this time, it was a comfort.

"Keeper and—you must be her Protector. I haven't seen your kind in our land for a long time," Itai said. His gaze found the weaponry in Ammun's hands. His eyebrows rose in amusement, and then finally, he held out his hands. "Oh, no, I have come to warn you. Not hurt you. I give you my word."

Ammun didn't drop his knife. His expression was unchanging as he rolled his wrist and adjusted his grip.

"What is it you have come to tell us, Warrior of the Abaddon?" Ammun asked. His tone was formal and commanding, like the Abaddon's had been. The warrior must have been thinking the same thing, for he flinched, but he was quick to regain his composure.

"Your brother and the Abaddon want to destroy the borders between Zarcane and Earth," Itai said. "They'll set loose the dark Fae creatures, and it will take only moments for them to rid the Earth of the humans. It's happening already. The borders are weak. The Earth's people are dying."

"As a loyal warrior, is it not your duty to protect the Abaddon, not put her in danger? Why are you coming to us with a warning?" Ammun questioned. I could still see the tension between his shoulders.

"There are many of us who have tired of the Abaddon's rule. She's a *cruel* leader," he spat out. A hard look passed over his eyes as he said this. "We never wanted the destruction of the humans. We never wanted her rule, but we had no choice." He stopped, noticing the skeptical look etched on to Ammun's face. He turned to me this time. "Keeper, I saved your life. I warned you about the food, remember?"

Ammun looked at me for confirmation of this fact. I nodded, trying to read his expression. It had never been easy to tell what Ammun was thinking, but I could guess. Right now, his face gave away nothing, and I wondered what he was contemplating.

"Warrior, if you are truly what you say you are. We will need your help," Ammun said. "We will need more men like you. We will need as many men as the Abaddon has to defend herself. Maybe more."

"We would be honored to stand by you."

"Good. Assemble an army."

I watched Itai nod automatically. He was about to gallop away, but he hesitated, turning back to us. "Forgive me, but what is it, exactly, that you intend to do?"

"I intend to give the Keepers a fighting chance," Ammun replied.

"But what of my people?" Itai's eyes were wide with worry.

"Trust me. That is all I ask. Your people will come out the better for it."

Itai finally nodded again, but it was a reluctant nod, not like the one before. He turned and left us, knowing the conversation was over.

"I am going to pay a visit to my brother at the Red Court. I need to get the amulet back, and I'll help your sister. Trust me. You just need to get the woman you were with."

"Calliel? How is she going to help?"

"She's more than what she seems," he said, playing with the bracelet around his wrist.

"Is this your way of admitting that she's not a demon?" I asked with a slight smile.

"We'll see where her loyalties lie," he replied, finally looking up at me.

"I know you. You wouldn't risk bringing one more demon into a land overflowing with them. I'll let you go alone, but promise me one thing."

"What?"

"That you'll be careful."

"It takes a lot to kill an angel. You humans are quite fragile." He winked at me and took off, his wings beating the air around him. Was this always how he was going to leave me? Me, chained to the ground, and him, free to fly across the sky.

Twenty-Eight

Farid

I stared blankly out of the window. The Abaddon had promised me a home here once I destroyed the amulets. I would get my own room. I would eat to my heart's content. I would have everything I needed and wanted. I had never even imagined that one day I would have so much comfort in my life.

"And you're sure they'll come for him?" the Abbadon's voice rang out. Everything that came out of her mouth was deceivingly beautiful.

"Yes, I'm certain of it, Your Highness. They can do as little as we can without the other Keeper. They will come, and when they do, we'll have both the amulets. We'll smash them and the borders will cease to exist!" Kasim replied.

Gazing up at the sky outside, I ignored them as best I could. Regardless of the Abaddon's promises, for now, I was a hostage. There was no other way to put it. They had taken my amulet. The only reason they hadn't locked me up in a room was because I could go nowhere without the amulet.

"I should mention that I have the other Keeper's sister in a cozy little room upstairs. She'll need a savior too," the Abaddon lilted.

"I should think they would be more inclined to hurry then," Kasim replied, smiling.

I stopped staring. Shock rippled through my blood. Isra mentioned that the Abaddon had taken her sister, but I had paid no mind to her then, blinded by my hatred. I couldn't believe this woman was using a child as a pawn in her game—a child who really didn't deserve to suffer. A child who could have been Maya. How could I let her do this? How could I side with her on this?

Outside, I saw a bird flying toward the palace. A big, white bird. It was coming closer fast. It was too big to be a bird, I realized.

"I'm going to take a walk," I mumbled, standing up.

The two of them didn't even bother to glance at me.

I found my way into the dim kitchen. There was a small wooden door there, used by the servants, but there were no servants around, going in or out. I turned the handle. Unsurprisingly, it was locked. Beside it was a circular window. Small . . . but not small enough that it wouldn't let me pass through if I got it open. I peeked through it first, wiping the fog away with the sleeve of my shirt, but even so, I could see nothing of what was outside.

Undoing the latch, I pushed the window open. The angel looked back at me expectantly. He had landed exactly where I guessed he would, beside the only door that had no guards posted outside. He raised his eyebrows, trying to read my next move.

"Come on," I said, moving away from the window to give him room to come through.

He didn't need to be told twice. He pulled himself to the ledge and squeezed through the window's opening, moving his body like a worm. He pushed a little more and when he didn't budge, I realized we had overestimated the size of the window. He was stuck.

I heard footsteps approaching. I had to get him out. I pulled at his arms as he wrapped his wings tight around his torso. I felt him move and suddenly, we were both barreling into the tiled floor. My back hit the ground right in front of a pair of tanned feet. A silver anklet rested just above an *L* shaped tattoo on the woman's left foot.

She yanked me up by the collar of my shirt with surprising strength. Her calloused fingers brushed my neck. When I was on my own two feet, I noticed that I was easily more than a few inches taller than her. She was young, but her back was bent. She certainly did not look like a fighter, yet she seemed ready to try her luck.

"Let me go," I said carefully, measuring my words and looking for any sign in her expression to show that she would let me go. This woman looked almost human, but her teeth were sharpened to points no human could have. She was another demon servant of the Abaddon. I would give her three seconds to move before I hit her, I decided.

Ammun crept up behind her, reaching for something on the side of his leg. "You *will* move out of his way," he hissed.

"I will do no such thing. I am loyal to the Abaddon, and I will not let you pass." She squared her shoulders and stayed put in front of me, but she was also turning to fight Ammun. It was futile courage since she couldn't possibly beat us both.

I didn't expect Ammun to do what he did next. He spun the knife in his hand and rammed the hilt into the woman's head. As she fell, I caught her in my arms and gently placed her on the floor.

Twenty-Nine

Isra

I was back in Kasim's apartment when I passed through the doorway. Without the smoke distorting it, I realized that his home was one that might actually have been nice to live in if he had only done a little cleaning up.

I found my way to the hospital eventually. No one saw me slip into Zaffirah's room. My fingers combed Zaffirah's hair away from her face. I avoided, as best I could, looking at the white pallor her skin had taken on. Instead, I leaned close to her ear.

"Zaffirah, get up. I need you," I whispered. "Please."

I shut my eyes for a moment, searching for my sister's energy—searching for her soul. I pushed every materialistic thought away. I let the world slip and searched for my sister's life, because I knew that as long as the machine beside her beeped, she was alive, and she would come back to me.

"Isra!" Rhiya called. She jolted me out of my head and back to reality. I opened my eyes to see Calliel beside her. Her arms brushed mine as she came closer and pressed her palms on either side of Zaffirah's head. She had her eyes shut, and her body went rigid.

"What is she doing? Stop!" I yelled. My breath caught in the back of my throat and panic prickled over my skin. I thought I would never agree with Ammun about the nature of this woman, but now I knew that, despite everything, his words had somehow gotten to me, and as a result, Calliel was losing my trust.

Rhiya held my wrists back. "Stop. She's helping her. Look."

Thirty

Farid

"If you plan to help me, I would much appreciate it, but if you don't, please just tell me now so I can knock you out and be done with it," Ammun said carefully, eyeing me. Veins, like cracks, coated the purple bags underneath his eyes. He was too worn out to even move his lips into a proper scowl.

I couldn't blame him for wanting to beat me up. "I want to help," I replied. "You'll need me. I know where they're keeping her sister."

"And the amulet? Do you have it?"

I looked down, shuffling my feet before shaking my head.

"Okay, but you do know how to find it, right?" he asked, breathing deeply.

I knew the answer he wanted was not the one I had, so I said nothing, but he quickly understood what my silence meant. I bit the inside of my cotton-tasting mouth, frustrated. How was it that I still knew so very little about my supposed destiny? Why was I so bloody useless?

"We'll get the girl, and then the find the amulet," Ammun muttered. I could hear the disappointment in his voice, even though his face remained neutral.

Before I could even nod in agreement, he snuck out of the kitchen, gesturing for me to follow. He pressed his body close to the walls. The guards wouldn't stop me, but I couldn't say the same for Ammun. I was fairly certain it would end badly for him if he was caught. The Abaddon had no reason I could think of to keep him alive. He was a prickly thorn in the beautiful rose that was her plan, and he needed to be trimmed. I prayed silently that no one would notice him and realized I didn't want his life on my hands. In fact, I didn't want any life on my hands, not truly.

I stopped before the spiral staircase and touched the golden banister. I pointed upward and Ammun nodded. "Go. I'll follow," he mouthed.

I ran, taking two steps at a time. When I got to the landing, I turned toward the corridor. As soon as I did this, I knew instantly which room the Abaddon had locked Zaffirah in. It was the only room with guards. On either side of the painted white door were wraith-like men. Their bones glowed under their skin.

I stepped back quickly, bumping into Ammun. He gave me a questioning look.

"One of us will need to distract them," I whispered.

"Leave it to me," he muttered.

Before I could stop him, he started flying. He rose toward the ceiling ever so quietly; even I had trouble believing he wasn't simply an illusion. Floating above the guards, he reached for the glowing candles in the glass chandelier.

One of the wraiths looked up. "You!" it hissed.

Ammun grabbed the candle and flew toward the other end of the corridor. The wraiths followed him, extending their arms above their heads in an attempt to catch him. They'd abandoned their posts.

Seeing my chance, I bolted for the door. I turned the handle and to my surprise, it opened easily.

Zaffirah was on the ground in the middle of the opulent room. She had wrapped her arms around her knees and by her slick, tear-stained face, I knew she had been crying.

She looked up at me and narrowed her eyes, but as recognition flooded her, she relaxed. Despite this, she made no attempt to rise. Instead, she shut her eyes and lowered her head to her knees. Her small frame shook violently as she began crying again. I quickly came to her, and as I knelt on the ground, I touched her elbow.

"You're okay. I'm going to help you get back," I murmured, trying to calm her.

She raised her head and shook it. "You can't help me. I can't go back," she wailed.

I wiped away her tears with the back of my hand. "I'll bring you home. Trust me. I just need the amulet."

I heard a sharp shriek from outside, and I knew Ammun had set the wraiths on fire. A moment later, he stepped over the broken door and scanned the room. A dark hole was burned into his shirt, but he was otherwise unharmed.

"The Abaddon keeps the amulet with her at all times," he said.

"How do you know that?"

"I got that information *before* I burned them," he muttered. "I'm open to suggestions if you have a plan," he added.

Before I could say anything, the Abaddon flounced into the room. Beside her was Kasim, and behind her were at least ten wraiths. Fire glowed in her eyes as her red lips turned up in a smile. "Looking for this?" she asked, holding the amulet tauntingly in her small hand.

Suddenly, her cruel, smiling eyes widened in shock. She dropped the amulet and it fell at Zaffirah's feet, beside me. I had hardly moved to retrieve it before it emitted a flash of white light and submerged Zaffirah completely. I had to shield my eyes from the brightness. Once it dulled, I could see that Zaffirah was no longer there.

Thirty-One

Isra

Calliel hadn't removed her hands from Zaffirah's temples. She bowed her head and whispered into her ear.

"Deala Roma Fae," she said. I wouldn't have heard if I wasn't sitting as close as I was to Zaffirah.

Rhiya maintained her grip around my wrists. It wasn't hurtful or violent, but there was a gentle firmness in the way her fingers curled around my hands, holding me back.

Before I could yank her off me, the white bulb above us buzzed and grew brighter in the ceiling. The room was suddenly dipped in a strange, white light for barely a few seconds before the colors returned to their natural state.

"What was that?" I asked, trying to keep the fear I felt out of my voice.

"Look at her eyes," Rhiya murmured, almost in a trance.

I looked back at Zaffirah and this time, I saw. Zaffirah's eyelids twitched. It was the slightest of movements. Something you wouldn't see if you weren't looking for it. I reached for Zaffirah's hand.

"Zaffirah?"

Seconds passed before I felt the squeeze from her hand and heard her say: "I'm here, Isra." Her voice was a soft, sweet lullaby.

"Are you all right?" I asked, taking her into my arms.

"I'm okay," she said, smiling.

I turned to Calliel. "All this time, you knew how to help her, but you didn't. How could you? I trusted you." My voice was dead. I had run out of the energy required to be angry. I was shocked. The feeling simmered underneath my skin as I came to terms with what I was seeing. The uncomfortable silence pressed in on me, and the longer Calliel did not speak, the more betrayed I felt.

"Isra, I'm sorry—"

"What are you, anyway? A demon?" I demanded.

Calliel held up her hand to silence me and sighed. "The Abaddon is my sister," she said. I could see in her eyes that she wished it unsaid. No, not unsaid, but untrue. She didn't like the fact, and why should she? It was obviously nothing to be proud of, and she was rightly ashamed.

I glanced at Calliel's protruding cheekbones and her full lips. They would have once been beautiful. As beautiful as the Queen's own features. Their eyes, too, were strikingly similar despite their colors. But there was wisdom and sadness behind Calliel's violet irises.

"I was the Queen of the Angels . . ." she said, when I made no attempt to say any more. "I was banished from Zarcane because I fell in love with a human soul. He was a dreamer, and when night came, when the borders were weak . . . he visited our land. Every day our bond became stronger, until I followed him back to your world. I didn't realize the consequences of my actions. I was young and in love. That was all that mattered. I begged the Keepers for more time, but virtuous as they were, they knew they had to seal the borders as soon as possible. So I left with him to Earth."

I laughed silently. A few days ago, I wouldn't have known at all what that feeling—love—was like, but now I did, and wished with great regret that I didn't. It could build you up higher than you had ever been, taller than any skyscraper, and then, without warning, yank the foundations out from beneath you so you would crash and never think to rise again.

Calliel continued her story. "When I tried to go back to Zarcane, I couldn't. So I lived here, and I married the man. I prayed for forgiveness from God. He took my powers and my wings as penance, but he granted me his forgiveness. He asked me to guide the Keepers to their true path, and I tried as best I could," she explained.

Now, I understood why Ammun had been so against this woman. She had dropped everything—all her responsibilities—for a man. It was because of her that Zarcane was now under the rule of the murderous Abaddon. I also understood the reason Ammun had pulled back after kissing me. I caught Rhiya's gaze and another question very nearly made its way to my lips, but Calliel beat me to it.

"Rhiya is our daughter. Everything angelic was taken away from me, and I became like you. A human. He died in a car crash. He was driving, and I was in the passenger seat. Though the shattered glass from the windshield didn't leave many scars, it took away my vision. I lost my sight with his death, but I saw it as a blessing that was protecting me from viewing tragedy again. I realize how silly that thought is now. I don't know how I was able to help your sister. My powers shouldn't exist. I never tried to use them before . . . not on Earth."

I snapped out of the temporary shock. We didn't have time for this. Ammun was still there, at the Abaddon's ghastly palace, and while I was reliving Calliel's memories, he could be hurt or even . . . as much as I hated to admit it, dying. I had to help him. Now.

"It doesn't matter. We have to go. I need you to come with me. We need to go back."

"I . . . I can't. I was banished," Calliel mumbled.

"You can't use your powers either, but here you are, doing just that. Does that count for nothing?" I cried. Calliel sat still and avoided my intent gaze. "Please," I begged.

She finally nodded. "Okay . . . but I don't know if I'll be able to pass through."

"You will," I said with conviction. Relief uncoiled within me. I knew I couldn't help Ammun alone. I knew I couldn't convince Farid to do the right thing alone. I needed her, and Ammun knew she would be helpful. "Hold my hand. Hurry!"

I held my palm face up, suspended in the air. Rhiya touched her hand with mine first. "I'm coming," she said. I looked pleadingly at Calliel. Maybe Rhiya coming would help her decision.

Zaffirah raised herself on the bed and leaned over as well.

"Not you," I muttered.

She looked at me with her big, brown eyes. "I want to help," she said softly.

I shook my head furiously. I was not letting her go back there.

"I want to come," she blurted.

I turned my back toward her, knowing it was for the best. I hoped she would be too tired to put up a fight. She tugged at my shirt, begging. I tried my best not to look at her; instead, I maintained my gaze on Calliel.

Mentally, I was forcing her hand upon our joined palms, but I couldn't force anyone to do anything. She looked up, and for a moment, I thought she would never do what I wanted her so desperately to, but she did. Streamers of joy burst within me. Before she could change her mind, I pulled out the amulet, shut my eyes and yelled the words that were hanging on the edges of my lips.

"Deala Roma Fae!" The ethereal coils of white light appeared in a hazy mist, slowly forming the archway of the door. "We have to step through it. Rhiya, go," I instructed.

I watched Rhiya's eyes widen with wonderment. The doorway almost looked as though it had some kind of pull on her. I remembered the allure it had had for me the first time I stepped through. It must have been similar for Rhiya. With her mouth hanging open, she walked through the doorway. It was Calliel's turn now. I watched her, trying to guess at what she was thinking, but her face revealed nothing.

"I can't," she mumbled. I saw tears glisten in her eyes, and I felt sorry for her. I wanted to make her pain disappear, but there was nothing I could do. I couldn't do anything when my father died. I couldn't do anything when my mother went insane. I couldn't even help my sister when she was snatched. I hated this feeling of helplessness. I met Calliel's gaze and watched as it wavered from side to side.

"You can," I said. Her unseeing, indigo eyes met mine, and for a moment, I felt as though she could really see me. I felt as though the sound of my voice had comforted her enough to make her agree to come. She nodded silently and we stepped through the doorway. As it disappeared behind us, fading into nothingness, I tied the amulet around my neck with a tight knot.

Thirty-Two

Farid

"Seize him," the Abaddon hissed.

Kasim was at his brother's side in less than a second. He held Ammun's arms behind his back, yanking them up so hard that he let out an involuntary moan of pain. Ammun kicked Kasim and he fell back, unable to maintain his hold. I noticed for the first time how weak Kasim's wings looked. I could see knobby bones across the top edge and the feathers that were once there seemed to be falling away.

Kasim rose, ready to seize Ammun once again, but two wraiths had beaten him to it. Ammun struggled against them, but soon realized, as I did, that even if he did get free it would be useless. His exit was blocked by the Abaddon.

Kasim narrowed his eyes and grinned. "No way out, is there, brother?"

Ammun refused to look at him and in return, Kasim punched him. The heavy thwack filled my ears and I shuddered, hoping Kasim hadn't broken his jaw.

"Look at me when I'm talking to you, brother," he snapped.

Ammun looked this time, and he looked hard. "I look at you and I see a demon whose wings are slowly being ripped off his body." He nodded toward the fallen feathers.

Kasim circled him and then, with lightning speed, he beat Ammun's wings. He kicked and punched and slapped and scratched. Ammun's wings thrashed him violently, sending gusts of wind throughout the room, but Kasim didn't stop till his arms sported fresh cuts, intertwining with each other on his skin.

"I don't need wings," he gasped out, breathless.

If Kasim beat me like that, I would last only a few minutes. I shuddered at the realization. It was the first time I was afraid to start a fight.

The Abaddon now turned her gaze to me. "Come closer," she instructed. Her voice rang out around me, pulling me toward her.

I approached her carefully, trying to predict her next move. She watched me, and then raised her hand and stroked my face with her nail. "You're a pretty boy. I don't want to hurt you. We both want the same thing, do we not?" she said.

I nodded quickly, suddenly eager to please her. I was as good as dead if she realized I no longer intended to do what I had agreed to.

"Humans are cruel creatures. They need to be taught a lesson, don't they?"

I nodded again, more forcefully than before.

"You'll help me, won't you?" She pursed her lips and blinked her lovely blue eyes.

I hesitated.

She stared at me intently, waiting. Her expression was soft, almost pitiful.

"Of course," I said.

I barely heard Ammun's scoff of disbelief from behind me as the room suddenly overflowed with the Abaddon's joyful laughter. She clapped her hands together, smiling wide. Then she leaned toward me and pressed her lips to my cheek. It was a touch as soft as a butterfly landing on my skin.

"Yes, of course," I repeated.

Thirty-Three

Isra

"Isra! Glad to see you!" Dearg whirled into my chest as soon I got through the door of light. I peeled him off me and narrowed my eyes. Beside him was Farid's little Maya. Her hair fell over her face, partially covering one side, and her arms were stained with grime.

"How did she get here?" I asked.

"Found her walking around. Then I found you," Dearg grumbled.

I looked back at the girl. She was lost in her own thoughts. "Maya, are you okay?" Her head snapped up. There was no recognition in her eyes. She didn't remember me. I wondered if she knew where she was.

"There were bugs. They hurt me. I lost my doggy. Have you seen my doggy? I'm looking for my doggy. Do you know where he is?" she asked. Her eyes danced around. She stared past me. I remembered the little puppy that had hidden behind her and helped her trick the woman so Farid could steal her money.

"The Abaddon's creatures attacked her," Dearg explained.

"Is she . . . ?" I couldn't bring myself to say the word. I didn't want another person to be dead because I hadn't completed my duty.

Confirming my fears, Dearg nodded. My stomach dropped a thousand feet, and I suddenly felt like I had been cut open and stuffed with straw.

"Keeper," a husky voice called.

I instantly recognized Itai's deep tone and turned. My jaw hung open and I shuddered, taken aback. Itai didn't stand alone. Behind him were almost a hundred centaurs armed with shields and swords. An army. Just as he had promised. Surrounding the centaurs were people made of crystals, the size of small children. The sunlight shone through them and gave them bodies in the colors of the rainbow. Their arms ended in sharp shards.

"These are the Crystal Creatures, they'll fight with us," Itai said. "Leave the child be for now."

He glanced at Calliel with her arm around Rhiya and his eyes widened with shock as he took every inch of her in. He bowed his head, but didn't drop to one knee as he had done for the Abaddon.

Calliel approached him slowly. "Itai, it has been a long time. How is young Orion?" she asked with a slight smile.

His eyes turned as dark as the city sky at night. "Dead," he muttered. His tone was accusing and cruel, directed at Calliel. She blanched and backed away from him.

I looked at them both. "The Abaddon . . ." I mumbled out loud when I finally put two and two together.

"Killed him," Itai said, louder this time.

It wasn't hard to believe Calliel's sister had killed Itai's son or brother. Whoever Orion was, he was obviously someone very close to Itai, and judging by the number of warriors that stood behind the centaur, he was only one amongst the many that the Abaddon had no doubt hurt. That was the real reason Itai had been helping me. He wanted to destroy the Abaddon for her carelessness with the lives of his people, and he wanted to avenge Orion's death.

Itai then glanced in my direction, ignoring what I had blurted out.

"Where is your Protector?" he asked.

Guilt hit me. Distracted by the sight of Maya and thoughts of this Orion, I had forgotten about Ammun . . . he had been pushed into some remote corner at the back of my mind.

"He—he left—he went to the Red Court," I mumbled. I saw Itai tense up.

"They will kill him. Keeper, we must leave now. Get on my back. Ayla, take the girl." Rhiya looked at me and before I could answer her stare, I felt the warrior grab me and place me on his back. I realized that I was glad he didn't waste any time asking for my permission. I wanted to get to Ammun as fast as I could.

Calliel stood still. Her eyes were shut. There was a flicker behind her back. Sparkles of kaleidoscopic light. The brightest was an electric magenta. It was the perfectly colored pigment between the deepest sea blue and ripest cherry red. The smell of sweet lavender drifted in the air as slivers of gossamer wings arched above Calliel's head. They glowed a pure white, tipped with smears of purple. I stared in awe as they trembled with overwhelming power. I wasn't the only one. Around me, the creatures couldn't help but gaze at her beauty. Her wings carried her up into the air. Millimeters at first. Then centimeters. Then meters.

"Go," she instructed.

Itai didn't hesitate. Either he was too used to taking instructions, or he couldn't bear to stare any longer at the woman he blamed for the death of his son. "Hold on tight," Itai whispered.

I looked one last time at Dearg. His arm was around Maya, who leaned on his shoulder, staring with empty eyes. Dearg's lips stretched in an encouraging grin. I returned the smile before Itai turned his back on them both and started galloping.

I tried to keep my body from bouncing as Itai gained momentum.

"Are you just going to charge her palace? Do you have a plan?" I yelled over the pounding of hooves.

"Our plan is to charge," Itai yelled back.

In minutes, the Abaddon's tall gates rose before us, manned by a number of guards. From behind Itai, arrows flew, stabbing the guards at the door. These ones weren't centaurs like Itai, nor were they made of crystal. They were skeletons plastered with silver, translucent skin. Their bodies shimmered with blood as they fell to their knees. I screamed as one came close enough for me to touch. The arrows had missed him. Itai pulled a dagger from his side and shoved it into the creature's body.

"You're safe on my back, Keeper," he roared. It provided little comfort, though. All I could see were bodies dropping around me.

From inside, someone raised the portcullis to allow us through.

Before I knew it, we were in the Red Court; but this time, when I looked up, the chandeliers didn't glow. The whole palace had been dipped in darkness. Itai continued to gallop, unfazed by the dimness. As the warrior entered another room, I noticed the bloody blaze of the other amulet at the far end. Basking in its light was the Abaddon, and beside her were Kasim and Farid. Pale feathers lay at Kasim's feet, and I could see pink slivers of skin on his wings. Those wings didn't look like they were in working condition anymore. I wondered if Ammun had done that to him.

"Desderia!" Itai yelled. I didn't realize it was the Abaddon he was addressing until she turned. The Abaddon regarded the warrior, but for the first time, she didn't look *down* upon him. Despite that, *afraid* was the last word that could have been used to describe her expression.

"I see that you no longer feel I'm worthy of the title of royalty." The Abaddon's features turned glacial as she mocked him.

"You lost that title the moment you started killing our people," Itai answered coolly, unaffected by the Abaddon's words.

"Is that so?" She raised one eyebrow, smirking.

The warrior ignored the Abaddon's question. "Where is the girl's Protector?" he asked. His hand touched the quiver of arrows behind his back. It was a comfort to him to know that it was there, and he could draw his bow any moment that he needed to.

"He's right here; don't you see him? A little light should help your poor vision." The Abaddon laughed. It was a laugh that was intended to make the warrior feel uncomfortable, and I could see that it succeeded in doing exactly that. Itai fidgeted, his hands stroking his bow.

The Abaddon snapped her fingers and flames leapt onto the wicks of the candles surrounding Ammun. His hands and legs were bound tight with twine. His wings hung limply behind him. I gasped, unable to hold in my shock. I shouldn't have wasted so much time getting to him.

"Let him go!" I yelled, rage blurring my vision.

"Now, now. Control your temper, and maybe I'll think about it," she teased. Fury bubbled within me. "Maybe we can strike a deal. Hmm? What do you say?" she ventured. I pushed away the instant notion to agree with whatever she demanded of me and glanced again at Ammun's crumpled form.

"Oh, my dear sister, don't patronize the girl," Calliel breathed. She waltzed in, with white, winged beings behind her. More angels, I guessed. She had her own army to support her.

The Abaddon froze. "What are you doing here? You were banished!" she fumed, when she had finally recovered from shock. "Where is that human of yours? You ran away with him. You left!"

"Gone—his soul is at peace," Calliel murmured. I saw hurt and guilt flash in her eyes. She shook her head—shaking whatever thought she was having away. "I want you to step away from the amulet," she said, her tone steely. Seconds passed. "Please." It was an afterthought that was obviously futile. One kind word would not stop the Abaddon.

"I hope you are not under the illusion that I will do as you've asked."

"No, I am not. But a part of me still hopes you will. I ask you only for your own good."

"Of course you do," the Abaddon grumbled. "You know what? I'm getting bored. Give me the Keeper and leave." She made a *shooing* motion with her hand. When no one moved, she smirked and twisted her wrist. Kasim stepped back, the shadows enveloping him. I realized that the motion with her wrist had been a signal. Where was Kasim going?

"If you don't give her to me, I'll have to take her by force, Calli," she threatened.

"You will do no such thing."

"Don't be so sure of that." The Abaddon raised her hand and snapped her fingers again.

After that, everything happened so fast. I was surprised that I could see it. Kasim lunged out of nowhere in a whirlwind of beating wings. He lifted me off the warrior's back and flew out of reach. His biceps tensed as they clutched me. Calliel shot after him. Her wings shimmered with purple hues. I wondered if she had gotten her sight back with her angel wings, or if she was simply listening to the sound of Kasim's wings.

I elbowed his chest and kicked every part of him that I could reach. He swooped low and then his wings, struggling to hold him up any longer, dropped him from the air. They were in worse condition than Ammun's. Kasim's arms loosened around me. I braced myself for impact as I connected with the floor. Sharp bursts of pain rippled through my back. Scarlet bruises bloomed on my elbows. Beside me, a silver, slipper-clad foot tapped patiently and rhythmically. It was the Abaddon's foot. Kasim had dropped me right at her feet.

I heard the cold *slick* of weapons as the centaurs drew their swords and bows. Some of them had come running forward, led by the Abaddon's very own warrior. They were prepared to fight. They had always been prepared to fight, and the Abaddon had now, unintentionally, given them their cue to raise their weapons and charge.

"Stop!" the Abaddon yelled. Her confident grin fell when not one of the swords was returned to its sheath or arrows to their quivers. Not a single one of the centaurs faltered. Scowling, she reached toward me and tore the amulet off my neck. I tried wrestling it away from her fingers, but for a woman so lithe, she was surprisingly strong. Her other hand reached for Farid's amulet on a table beside her. I realized what she was going to do before she did it. She was trying to get leverage over them and destroying the amulets was the only thing she had left. The warriors finally halted in their tracks.

"Stop or you'll lose everything that you're fighting for," she threatened. "The moment these amulets touch, Earth will be destroyed. You do know that, don't you, dear sister?"

"I believe you are sorely mistaken, Desderia, but do try it."

I turned to Calliel, shocked. What was she doing? She was provoking her sister. She knew what was coming and she was willingly letting it happen. She was inciting it.

The Abaddon pushed the amulets together, expecting them to smash and destroy the borders, but they flew out of her hands, hovering out of her reach just before they were meant to touch. One of the two soared toward me and landed in my cupped palms. The other landed in Farid's. The Abaddon let out an exasperated cry.

"The decision will always be for the Keepers to make. Not me . . . or you," Calliel said, as though she was reciting a line that she had memorized especially for this day, to humiliate her sister.

"Keeper this, Keeper that. *Blah blah blah.*" The Abaddon motioned for Farid to come forward. He hesitated a little, but did as he was told. I could sense a new plan formulating in the Abaddon's pretty little head. From the intricate fold in the fabric around her waist, the Abaddon yanked free an ivory dagger. She placed it in Farid's hand and whispered words I couldn't hear in his ear. Farid glanced at me, his arms quivering, and he shook his head. The Abaddon stroked his dark hair and murmured a few more words in his ear. Again, he shook his head.

"It's the only way, my dear. You want to destroy the borders, don't you? You want the world to suffer, don't you? You pledged your loyalty to me, now do as I've asked," she said, louder this time. "Kill her."

"No. Stop," Ammun whimpered. They were the first words I'd heard escape his lips. I was surprised he could talk, but extremely glad he still had the slightest strength to speak. Every eye was on him now. "I'll do whatever you want me to. Just don't hurt her." Ammun tried to stand, wobbling clumsily. His arms and legs were still tied. He looked down at them, seeming to notice the twine for the first time.

"Looks like someone else is worried about the Keeper's *oh-so-precious* life. Oh, young Protector, are you worried about *your* life, or am I sensing a cupid's hand at work here? Oh, how I adore young love . . . destroyed, of course," the Abaddon said, looking at him in mock pity. "Farid, kill her!" she ordered.

The centaurs tensed and raised their swords, but they were now hesitant to attack. Farid was only a few feet in front of me. They'd never get to me fast enough. The boy that was once my closest friend was now going to kill me. I was going to die. It was going to be smooth and quick, like I had never been alive in the first place.

Farid raised the dagger above his head. I prepared myself for what I knew was to come. He was actually going to do it. I wasn't certain until that moment. His jade eyes were apologetic. His cheeks were wet from tears. One slid past his nose and into the corner of his mouth.

"Kill her!" the Abaddon yelled.

"I'm sorry," he whispered, reinforcing the expression on his face. I didn't want to look at him anymore. He was a pitiful sight, and I didn't want spend my last breaths pitying the boy who was going to kill me. To some extent, his hesitation was comforting. I was glad that it wasn't easy for him to simply slice the dagger through the air and into my body.

"If you're really sorry, you wouldn't do this," I snapped.

He reacted little to what I had said.

In the far corner of the room, Ammun had finally found the energy to move and break his bonds. He ran toward me, and with his wings extended, he formed a tent over my body. He was shielding me, leaving his own back exposed. I knew where the dagger would hit. I struggled underneath him. He was going to die for me. I couldn't let that happen. I pushed my palms against his chest, but he didn't move.

I heard a wet sound and then murmurs of shock filled the room.

"Ammun," I whispered.

"I'm okay," he replied. His breath was ragged, but when he rolled off me, I realized he hadn't been hurt. I could now see Farid. The front of his shirt was covered with a reflective, ruby stain. He had stabbed the knife into his own stomach. The gash was deep and already forming a pool of blood around him. Calliel landed on the floor beside him. Her hands worked quickly over his body. I couldn't see exactly what she was doing. I wondered whether or not it was working.

"Stupid boy. What a waste," the Abaddon muttered, and that was the last straw. The centaurs rushed forward. Out of nowhere came a few of the Abaddon's own warriors, the ones that had stayed loyal enough to defend her. The angels descended to fight them off. Where there was once only Calliel, now, there were about twenty that I could count, their colorful wings holding them up as they used their various weapons to shoot down the demons. I screamed as lifeless bodies fell from each sword. Arrows punctured limbs, slowing the creatures down. I wasn't sure which side was winning.

I saw creatures that were neither centaur nor angel— creatures that almost looked human, but were far from it. Some of them had claws for hands. There were a few with skin that glowed different colors, but the ones that were using their teeth as weapons scared me the most. They bit off fingers and chunks of skin.

The heavy clinks of metal as swords hit shields met my ears. For a moment, I was frozen in place, listening to that sound.

"*Sssssssssss.*"

Suddenly, the whole world fell silent.

"*Israaa.*"

I turned my head, searching for the source of the noise. A small, slender snake slithered toward me. It was the first time I had seen the creature. Its eyes were black pinpricks and there were circular markings on the side of its black head. I was struck with a sickening feeling, but, hypnotized by its appearance, I stayed focused on its every move. I caught glimpses of its forked tongue as it spoke.

"*Desssstroy the amulets, Isssraaa,*" it whispered. I reached over to touch the creature. My hand fell straight through it. Its body wasn't solid. It broke apart at my touch and a sharp buzzing filled the air around me. A dark cloud of black insects lingered above my head. Quickly, they began to land on me. I felt a searing pain as an insect bit into my knee. I shrieked and slapped it away. A bead of blood bubbled on the surface of my skin. Another shot of pain rippled from my neck. The insect had bitten me again.

"We killed your father . . ." they echoed. They weren't insects, I realized. They were like the Rose Flies, their wings attached to tiny human bodies.

What were they talking about? These creatures couldn't be the reason for my father's death. They couldn't. This death would have been worse than a bullet from a gun or the flames of a bomb. It would have been slow, gruesome, and unmerciful.

"Come now, my pretties. We need her to control the amulets, especially since boy wonder there is dead," the

Abaddon called. It took me a second to realize that her voice was directed at the creatures. There was not a hint of regret in her tone.

Instantly, the black beasts abandoned my body and approached her. The Abaddon yanked my arms and pulled me to my feet. I felt a breath of wind as Ammun appeared beside me, his wings tucked closed behind his back. The Abaddon raised her eyebrows and observed him.

"You take your job quite seriously, don't you, little angel?" When he didn't reply, the Abaddon turned to me instead. "Now then, it's quite simple. If you don't do exactly as I say, that girl over there will have nothing left to live for." I looked toward where she glanced, knowing what I would see. Farid had created a big enough distraction that one of her demons had managed to grab Rhiya. She was limp and unmoving as the demon held her in his arms carelessly.

"No! Let her go!" I yelled. "I'll do whatever you want. Please, let her go," I said, more calmly this time. Yelling only made me seem like a lunatic, and it pleased the Abaddon to see me so perturbed.

"No point, now, is there? She's unconscious, and she won't be able to walk. You do exactly as I say and I won't kill her, but if you don't, I will torture her until she wishes she were dead, and I will make sure that you are there to watch. Am I clear?"

I nodded.

"Good. Now, I know you're fond of your lovely little angel, but he will have to go." Her eyes narrowed and I could tell that this was a test. One wrong move and Rhiya would be in trouble. The demon wouldn't hesitate to do as the Abaddon had asked.

Ammun turned to me, his jaw set. The last thing he wanted to do was leave me with the Abaddon. I saw that clearly in the way he planted his feet firmly on the ground and stood close to my side.

"She can't hurt me. She needs me. Please, Ammun. You have to go," I pleaded. I knew he wanted to disagree, but what I said was true. I was now the only one left that could control the amulets. She really did need me or she would have no one. I wondered whom the amulets would go to if both Keepers were dead.

Dead, I thought. What happened to Kasim? I looked up, and in the far corner, opposite Rhiya and the demon, I saw him limping toward the door. Kasim was moving. He hadn't fallen down unconscious. *When the Keeper dies, it is our fault, and death is our punishment.* Those were Ammun's words. Farid couldn't be dead if Kasim was moving. The Abaddon hadn't noticed Farid yet, but she soon would if I didn't do exactly as she asked.

I looked to Ammun, trying to communicate with my eyes what I could not with words. He glanced to Farid and bent his head slightly in a nod. He now knew Farid was breathing.

"Go," I said again.

"Okay." He nodded before taking off.

I silently thanked him. I saw in his expression what he had really meant. He was going to protect me, and I would see him soon. This was just an act.

"Good job," the Abaddon scorned. "Now, let's get out of this dreadful place. They've ruined my palace." She pouted like a spoilt child and grabbed my wrist. Her silver nails dug into my veins. I let her drag me out to wherever she wanted to go with little resistance.

Thirty-Four

Farid

The blood seeped through my shirt. It started with a strange pressure, as though someone was pushing a fist into my stomach, but that pressure turned to fire in seconds. I doubled over, clutching my body, and fell to the ground. It felt like I hadn't just stabbed myself once, but multiple times, over and over again. The throbbing pulsed to the speed of my heartbeat.

"Look at me!" a woman yelled.

I looked up, trying to focus on the woman's violet eyes, but it was getting darker. I couldn't adjust my sight to the dimness. She shook my shoulders hard. My chin knocked against my chest, but I could see her again. Her deep, purple eyes, at least.

"You're going to be okay," she murmured, ripping something and wrapping it around my stomach. It was too tight, almost like another knife going into my body, making the wound in my stomach deeper.

I struggled against her, but my body was slow and sluggish. I couldn't even form words. From the corners of my vision, the darkness was stretching out its strange tendrils. It stretched and recoiled. Stretched and recoiled. Stretched and recoiled. The same thing happened countless times, blinding me.

I heard a sharp intake of air from the woman beside me. "My daughter," she whispered. A cool wind rushed over my face, and she was gone.

Someone else's arms went underneath me and I was lifted off the ground. The pain in my stomach exploded, sending shocks to every corner of my body. I gasped out, the metallic taste of blood in my mouth and shrill screams in my ears.

Thirty-Five

Isra

"Come," the Abaddon commanded.

She stepped gingerly between the bodies that were lying outside her gate, not once letting go of my arm. Her expression was more disgusted than shocked or saddened at the sight of the bodies, most of them her guards.

It was only a few minutes before we ended up by a small creek. The water bubbled, crashing into rocks, murmuring restlessly. An array of colorful fish from every sector of the rainbow swam toward the rippling surface.

"What do you want from me?" I asked. I was stalling quite poorly. However, it did seem to slow her down . . . if only slightly. She proceeded, to my relief, to answer my question.

"It's quite simple really. I want their destruction."

"Who's they?" I asked, feigning ignorance.

She stared at me, trying to catch me at my game. "The humans. Who else?" she snapped.

"Okay, so I destroy the amulets and they die. Then it's all over?"

"No, I want them to writhe in pain. I was an angel once. Did you know that? All demons were once angels. We didn't bow down to you silly humans, and He took away our powers. He took away our wings. Can you believe it? Us, made of fire, bowing down to you humans, made of mud! It was disgraceful," she mused.

"It doesn't sound that disgraceful to me," I muttered.

"Of course, you would say that. You are a human after all. I want you to open a permanent doorway so it's easier for my kind to slip through the realms. At the moment, only the little ones can do it."

"What will you give me in return?" I asked.

"My dear, you are in no place to negotiate. But you know what? There is something I can do for you. I'll spare that girl's life. Is that good enough?" she snorted with a smile. That smile, however, didn't last long. "Oww," she screamed, slapping her wrist.

There was a burst of silver glitter. I saw the ochre-colored liquid glisten as it fell from her hand in fat drops. She flinched again and smacked her shoulder. This time, she missed the bug. The creature hovered closer. The one I was looking at had peach wings. It was a Rose Fly.

"*We're helping you. Go, find her,*" the creature's melodious voice rang out. For a second, I just stood and stared. The creatures swarmed the Abaddon's body. Her sharp cries of pain sliced through the air.

Ammun appeared out of nowhere, snapped his fingers in my face, and broke the spell.

"Come on. I know where she is," he murmured. He began walking.

"Flying would be quicker," I pointed out, noticing his wings had healed. They were stretched out behind his back; white, pure, and powerful.

"You're right." He turned around and gave me a gentle push before lifting me on his back. I looked over his shoulder at the Abaddon's crumpled form. The creatures flew around her, pulling her hair and sinking their teeth into her skin. I didn't want her to die like that. My father had died like that.

Ammun seemed to have read my mind. He sighed. "Isra, they can't kill her. She's not human. They will only slow her down."

I nodded and held on tighter. The Abaddon opened her mouth and screamed. I shut my eyes. There was a gust of wind and I knew that we had taken off. The cool wind smothered me. I shivered and held tighter to Ammun. His body was comfortingly warm.

"Down there. Do you see her?" Ammun pointed. I looked toward where he was pointing. It was the rose garden that I had first seen when I entered Zarcane. Beside the roses, Rhiya was kneeling over something. Itai hovered beside her.

Ammun gestured toward Farid as his feet touched the ground. A piece of fabric had been tightly knotted around his torso to staunch the bleeding. Despite that, his blood had already stained the fabric. Drops fell from the makeshift bandage. Farid's eyes were shut, and his skin was tainted with a ghastly pallor. If it wasn't for the slight rising of his chest, I would've have thought that he was dead.

"He's alive," I sniveled. I had to say it out loud. I had to make it feel like it was truly real. "How did they get out of her palace?" I asked Ammun.

"You think a small, pathetic demon is any match for the once again great and powerful, Calliel? You think she would let anything harm her daughter?" he said, smirking. "She attacked it from behind and distracted. He dropped Rhiya. Itai grabbed her, and thanks to you, I grabbed Farid. Everyone else was a little preoccupied with the fighting, so we literally walked out the door and no one noticed," Ammun replied.

I nodded and then reached over Farid. I put my arms around his neck. His heart fluttered weakly underneath my chest. "I'm glad you're alive," I whispered in his ear.

"Oww," he murmured. His voice was hoarse. He opened his eyes and looked at me. He didn't have to say anything, but I saw a heartfelt apology in his eyes. That was enough for me. I didn't need any more. The look on his face was heart-breaking. He had been so convinced that he was doing the right thing by agreeing to destroy the borders with

Kasim and the Abaddon that he had never considered the consequences.

"It's all right. I forgive you," I replied. "I forgive you for everything. Just promise me you'll listen to me from now on."

His head bobbed up and down eagerly.

"Someone did a good job," I said, gesturing to his make-shift bandage.

"My mother dressed the wound as best she could," Rhiya explained. "He would have died if it wasn't for her." I didn't doubt that he would have. He still looked like he could go at any second.

"I'm glad she did," I replied. "But what about Kasim?"

"Kasim is weak now, but his life is connected to Farid's. As he heals, Kasim will get stronger. He ran. Calliel managed to save Rhiya, but she couldn't catch Kasim," Ammun replied.

I nodded. "And where is Calliel?" I asked.

"She went after her sister," Rhiya murmured. She looked like she was about to burst into tears.

"There's no point worrying about her. She'll be able to handle herself just fine," Ammun comforted, touching Rhiya's arm. He turned to me, sighing, when Rhiya pushed him away. "Do you have the amulets? Before you seal the borders, you and '*boy wonder*' over there are going to have to guide the lost souls back to Earth, or they'll be trapped here forever," he said.

I heard a heavy thrum at the amulet's mention. I felt in my pockets and there it was, just as I had tucked it. It had come back to me and then never left. I relished its feel, never wanting to let it go again.

"Where's the other one?" Ammun interjected. I reached into my other pocket, but I already knew that it wouldn't be there. I couldn't sense its presence.

Ammun glanced at Farid on the ground. He had shut his eyes again. The pain was wearing him out. If only Ammun would give him a sip of his blood. He was a Keeper too, right? The moment I had the thought, Ammun turned over his shoe and reached into its sole. I knew what would be there. I had seen him do this enough times. He brought out his knife. The blade reflected the sun's light.

"I don't know if it will work, but it's worth a try," he said. He dragged the blade across his palm and the silver dripped with a dazzling amber liquid. He passed me the knife, and I knew that convincing Farid to drink it was up to me.

"Farid . . ." I started.

"Mhhmm," he mumbled, wincing.

"I need you—I need you to drink—Farid, you have to drink his blood."

He took a deep breath. "What . . . did . . . you . . . say?"

"Angel blood heals," I squeaked.

"I've seen this before," he gasped out, to my surprise. His breathing had become heavier.

I didn't even have to convince him. He used his forefinger and thumb to wipe the sticky liquid off the knife. Ammun turned away at the look of disgust plastered on Farid's face. Frankly, I didn't expect him to drink it without making that face. I suppose I would have done the same, had I known what I was drinking. It made all the difference. The fact that it didn't look like human blood did help a little. Farid raised his fingers to his lips and paused.

"Don't think about it. Just do it," I urged.

His tongue stretched toward his finger and he licked the blood. As soon as he did, the rosy color returned to his face and the playful sparkle was back in his eyes.

Rhiya undid the knot of his bandage. Her slender fingers were careful and worked quickly. As she pulled the fabric away, I noticed that the blood smeared on his stomach no longer had a source. The angel blood had healed him as it had done me.

Farid pushed himself up easily. The blood had also given him a newfound energy. "Thank you," he said.

"It wasn't me. It was all him." I jerked my head toward Ammun.

Farid stared at Ammun for a second, and then cautiously approached him as though he expected to be hit. If he hadn't just stabbed himself, I would have thought he deserved it, but he had had enough for one day.

"I'm sorry. Thank you for helping me. It was . . . kind of you," Farid stammered.

"I didn't do it for you. We need the amulet back and because it's not here, you are going to have to learn to do your duty right. Call the amulet back to you," Ammun snapped. "I'm assuming you didn't store it in your pocket when you stabbed yourself."

Ammun's words worked. Farid turned to me for advice.

"I've never done it before," he said.

"It's okay. It's easy. The amulet will always come back to you. Wherever it may be, it will *always* belong with you. All you have to do is call it. In your head, listen for its sound. Okay?"

"I don't know if it'll work."

"It *will* work. Close your eyes."

His eyelids fell, and they creased with tension as he focused. He seemed to be having trouble. Knowing how to use the amulet had come easy to me, but I could tell it was harder for him. His fingers fiddled with a non-existent object on his lap.

"I see it," he exclaimed, his eyes still shut. He hadn't expected it to work. By "*I don't know if it'll work*" he had meant "*it is never going to work*."

"Now, hold it in your palms and open your eyes," I instructed.

His palms curled together and his green eyes flashed open. He pulled his hands apart and the amulet came into view, glowing scarlet, the silvers and golds merging into each other. Farid smiled the moment he saw it.

"I hate to say it, but I told you so," I teased. The corners of Farid's lips curled involuntarily, and he laughed.

Thirty-Six

Isra

Ammun brought us to a clearing deeper in the heart of the garden. Trees with ferns like hanging curtains surrounded a number of children.

"Have you seen him? My doggy? He'll be sad without me. He needs me," Maya whimpered. Her voice had grown tired. I could imagine her insistent tone forcing the others to go looking at some point, but now, her voice had become unsteady and soft. It had jumped a few octaves. Her hands were also shaking, and her eyes had filled with the hot, wet tears of hopelessness.

"Shhh," Dearg murmured, patting her hand.

"I want to go home!" Another child erupted in tears.

"I miss my Mummy."

"Where's my Daddy?"

The children's voices surged with a force of utter sorrow. Dearg went from child to child, whispering words of comfort in each one's ear. Most of the time, those words had no effect, but once in while a child's sobbing would cease, only to begin again a moment later. I was surprised that not one child seemed to be afraid of this heavy, stone creature.

"Dearg," I called. He looked up at me. Maya's face also curiously turned upward. She caught sight of Farid and bounded toward him. Her eyes glittered, this time with happiness rather than sadness. Farid returned the hug. He gently stroked strands of Maya's hair back and smiled down at her.

"What is she doing here?" he asked. The question was directed to no one in particular, and I couldn't bring myself to say anything.

"Maya must pass over," Dearg grumbled.

"What does that mean?" Farid turned to Dearg. "What do you mean she needs to pass over? She's not dead! She has nowhere to pass over to! Why would she have to pass over?"

Ammun took a step back. I put my hand on Farid's shoulder. "Farid . . ." I started.

"I'm bringing her back with me. She's not passing over anywhere," Farid snapped.

"Yes! I'll stay with Farid!" She grinned at him, as though nothing in this world could ever be wrong.

"You knew there was a possibility that she could be . . ."
Dead. I let the word hang, unsaid.

He pulled Maya toward him once again, and this time, it didn't look like he was ever going to let go.

"If the girl is dead, she must cross over," Itai repeated from behind him.

"No! I'm not going anywhere!" Maya wailed, her voice muffled by Farid's chest. She pulled away from Farid and though he clearly didn't want to, Farid let her go.

"All she does is cry. I just got her to hush, and then you come and make her cry again!" Dearg groaned, prodding me angrily. He knelt by the child and whispered in her ear. She ignored him and bawled louder. Her nose was red and her face, wet.

I glanced at the children surrounding her. There were about twelve of them. Some were fair with freckled skin, and there were others with dark, ginger hair. They were from all over the world.

"Are they all . . ." *Dead,* I wanted to say, but again, held back the word.

Dearg shook his head. "Dreamers, lost in this land, waiting to be taken home. Children like to dream."

A boy with feathered blonde hair tugged at my shirt. His eyes were puffed from crying and trails of tears had dried on his cheeks. "Will we, will we get . . . to . . . go . . . home now?" he sniveled.

"Yes, you will. All of you," Ammun answered for me.

The atmosphere instantly transformed. The children wiped away their tears. Some smiled a little. A few jumped up and wrapped their arms around Ammun. They all began talking at once, excited.

"How long have they been here?" I whispered.

"Some for months, and others only a few days," Dearg replied. "Isra must open the doorway and bring them back."

"Farid, it would make things easier if you helped her," Ammun cut in.

"I know," Farid murmured, but did not move from Maya's side.

"Any time today would be good," Ammun retorted. He glanced at Maya, still crying, and then softened his tone. "She's not going anywhere . . . for now."

Farid nodded and reluctantly placed his amulet down on the grass.

"Isra must place hers beside his," Dearg instructed. I approached Farid's amulet and knelt down, placing mine.

"As soon as the doorway opens, Isra and Farid must take the children through, one at a time. Child's soul must touch body to be accepted back into Earth," Dearg explained.

We both nodded.

"If doesn't work, or physical body is destroyed, child must come back," Dearg added. He said these words so softly that I was sure none of the children had heard.

Ammun and Rhiya gathered the children and assembled them like soldiers in a line. All of them but little Maya, who was still looking at Farid with starry eyes. I imagined them telling stories of this place to their parents, who would nod patiently, but pay no attention.

Farid held out his palm and I took his hand in mine. It was warm and comforting. Just like Farid's presence had always been for me. I saw Ammun grit his teeth at us.

"Ready?" Farid asked. His eyes bored into mine. I nodded, and together, we said the words.

"Deala Roma Fae!" we yelled simultaneously.

Our voices mingled and joined so completely that it sounded almost as though the noise had come from *one* person as opposed to two. Our energies wrapped into each other, and I was enveloped with the feeling of utter joy and peace. It was a feeling that I knew I wouldn't be able to explain, only share with Farid.

The glimmering white doorway appeared before us. It was bigger than the one we would have been able to create on our own.

"Go." Ammun nudged a boy forward. His sandy hair flopped over his left eye, and his thumb was in his mouth. He held back, afraid. I reached out to him.

"It's okay. It'll take you home. We'll come with you," I coaxed. He took half a step toward us. Then another. With my free hand, I gently urged him forward.

"We're going to go through this door, okay? It's the only way back home," Farid explained patiently. The little boy had taken a liking to Farid. He curled his fingers around Farid's wrist. Farid had a way with children that I obviously would never have.

"Are you ready?" Farid asked.

The boy nodded and allowed himself to be easily pulled through the doorway. I looked back at Ammun. He had an encouraging smile daubed on his face. I couldn't tell if it was real or fake.

The doorway brought us to a room that I had never seen before. A child's room. The walls were painted baby blue and on the ceiling were plastic stars that glowed a pale green in the darkness. The dark curtains matched the hardly visible blanket on the bed. There were so many stuffed animals that they took up more room than the sleeping body. A fluffy, brown bear gave us a blank stare with his button eyes.

The boy ran to the bear and circled him in his arms. "This is Penny," he introduced.

He hadn't noticed his look-a-like occupying the bed. There were machines connected to the body. One measured his heart-beat. They were the same machines I had seen attached to Zaffirah in the hospital. All this boy had to do was touch his physical body and everything would be okay again, I told myself. He would be back with his mother and father, happily at home.

Farid guided the boy closer to the bed. He finally noticed his twin and, with a curious look in his eyes, he poked the body. I suppose he had done it to check if he was real or not. A burst of white light consumed the little boy and his double. I shielded my eyes. It hurt too much to stare.

The light finally faded into nothingness and I spared one last glance at the boy in the bed. He was curled with his teddy, snoring peacefully. Eyelids closed against the dim light of his glow-in-the-dark stars. All the muscles in his face and body were completely relaxed. He looked like a newborn in its first seconds of slumber. He hardly moved, other than the quick rising of his chest with each intake of air. This was a boy who was completely oblivious to the day's turmoil.

"Let's go," I urged, turning my back to the boy. Farid pulled himself away and nodded. The doorway was still open and we easily passed through it, without hesitation. There was nothing else we could do for the boy.

Ammun was waiting at the other end, a girl with smooth, coffee-colored skin beside him. Her hair was a curly mess. It looked as though it hadn't been brushed in weeks. "Her name is Zaidi," Ammun introduced.

Farid knelt down before the girl so he could look her in the eye. "Hello, Zaidi," he said. The girl shook his hand, at first hesitantly, but the crazy smile on Farid's face soon had her cracking up. "We'll take you home, but you have to do as we say, okay?"

She nodded obediently. Farid was able to make every child feel at ease around him. When we had finally brought the last child home and there was no one but Maya left, he hugged the little girl again and made her laugh. They shared a bond as close as mine and Zaffirah's, even though they weren't related by blood.

He knelt down before her so he could look her in the eye. This time, the smile on his face was heartbreaking. He had accepted the fact that, in a few moments, his Maya would be well and truly gone. "Maya, my dear little Maya, I wish we could stay here together forever, but you need to cross over. This isn't a permanent place for little girls to live in."

"But, I don't want to go alone!" she cried. Little tears fell from her eyes and slid down her chin.

"Maya, the place where you're going to go when you cross over will be much better," Ammun broke in.

"But it won't have Farid *bhai*," she moaned.

"There will be other children to play with, though," Farid coaxed.

"I don't want other children. I want you!" Maya poked him to emphasize this.

"Oh Maya, I'll be there too, eventually. Just not yet."

"Are you sure?" Maya asked softly.

He hesitated for a moment before nodding. It was a lie that had to be told. Maya wouldn't have a physical place to go to once she crossed over, and when Farid crossed over too, he wouldn't really be Farid. He would be a soul that would simply join with God's, like Maya's would soon do—like my mother and every soul in the past centuries had—but she didn't need to know that.

"Okay, I'll go," she said finally.

The moment she said this, her skin turned translucent, and then completely transparent. She had no bones or veins or blood. She was made of nothingness. Her solid form faded from our sight.

Farid stared at the space where she had stood for a long time before whispering a soft goodbye and rubbing the wetness from his eyes. He shielded it so we wouldn't see what he was doing.

Thirty-Seven

Isra

Calliel descended at precisely that moment. Behind her were the centaurs and a few of the Crystal Creatures with shattered limbs. Some were limping. The centaurs' hair was matted with sweat and blood. A lot of them had bandages similar to Farid's.

Rhiya ran to her mother and pressed into her body, unembarrassed. Calliel stroked her head and smiled at the show of affection.

"What happened your sister? Is she dead?" Ammun asked, interrupting their moment.

"She's gone . . . that's all that matters," Calliel replied, pulling away from her daughter.

"What do you mean by gone?" Ammun pressed.

"Her body and soul were shredded. She's weak now, so she won't be back for a long time, and when she's back, we'll destroy her again," she said simply, as if that put an end to it.

"So there's only one thing left to do," I remarked.

"Yes. The borders. You have a choice to make—" Calliel started.

"Haven't we been over this?" I asked.

"No, there is something you don't know. You can choose whether to stay here or go back, because you are the Keepers. Even when the borders shut. The amulets will, of course, go back to Earth to new Keepers."

I looked at Ammun. "What about you? Do you have a choice?"

"It's either here or up there. That's where my home is, Isra. I can't go back to Earth. I have done my duty," Ammun mumbled. His head was bent, and he was staring at the ground as though he had seen something far more interesting there than this conversation. He couldn't even look at me. Well, he'd be happy to know I was leaving. My place was not here, just as his was not on Earth. My place was by my sister.

"Okay then," I said loudly. "I'm going home, and I would love to have you come with me." I glanced at Farid and he nodded, to my relief. I wasn't going to lose all my friends.

Itai stepped forward, blocking our path. "There's one more thing that needs to be done, and it would be our honor to have the Keepers present for such a momentous occasion." Once again, the warrior's voice had taken on the same commanding tone that he had used when he first met me. The only difference was that it didn't scare me anymore.

"What is it, Itai?" I asked.

"Considering the state of our current ruler, we will need a new queen."

"I understand. It would be our honor to see your new queen crowned." I smiled at Calliel. She would get her position back once more. She would get another chance to be the great and loyal ruler that she never was.

Itai knelt before her on one knee, bowing his head. I had seen him do this before, but this time, his stance seemed more sincere. As it should be, he was now bowing of his own free will rather than from fear.

"My Queen," he said.

The other centaurs copied Itai's motion. Then the Crystal Creatures went down on their knees too. Calliel smiled, and I knew that, in that moment, she was finally sure she had done the right thing by coming here. She placed a hand on the warrior's shoulder and told him to stand.

To my surprise, Itai shrugged her hand off his shoulder.

"Forgive me, but it was not you I was addressing," he said. Then, he looked expectantly at Rhiya.

She turned from him to her mother, choosing what to

do next carefully. "Please rise," she said finally. It was a strong voice, bigger than the girl it had come from.

The creatures rose obediently, row by row. Rhiya now had a full army of willing servants at her disposal.

The smile had fallen from Calliel's face, but the love she held for Rhiya was too great for her to show any jealousy. Instead, her eyebrows were raised in question.

"We need a ruler who will be fair to all factions in our land. A ruler who will not simply abandon us," Itai replied, taking in her look. What he had said had not been malicious. It was simply a cold fact. But Calliel looked appropriately abashed.

"Your daughter has neither the pride of an angel nor a demon. She will have you to guide her against the mistakes made in the past and us to protect her against the Abaddon's creatures should some of them have survived," he continued.

"You have made a wise decision," Calliel stammered. I could see her trying to hide her true opinion on the matter. Her lips almost seemed to frown, but she turned them into an emotionless straight line just in time.

I couldn't help but think about how Rhiya would learn to lead so many. She was soft spoken and, being human, weak. She couldn't compare to the strength of the Abaddon or Calliel. But she was also clever and, though she painted a picture of utter obedience to her mother, I knew she would make her own decisions. She had the potential to be the best thing that had ever happened to these people. Despite whatever Calliel thought, the creatures had made a good decision.

Thirty-Eight

Isra

After Itai finally allowed us to leave, Ammun led us back into the darkness of the Cave of Songs. The sweet voices drifted around me. I had been here enough times that I could now walk without stumbling over the uneven terrain. I kept my distance from Ammun, and he from me. This was going to be the last time I saw him. The knowledge of that fact burned into my brain. I watched him climb effortlessly over the fallen rocks. The clearing of light where the cave drawings had been carved had come too soon.

I wanted more time to simply stare at Ammun. What was wrong with me?

I heard fingers snapping, and I was instantly pulled out of my head.

Ammun stood in front of me, irritated. I had gotten that expression from him way too many times. The lines on his face hardened. "Were you listening to anything?"

"Sorry," I muttered, shaking my head.

"It doesn't matter. I think you know what to do, anyway," Ammun said. I found it strange how he had almost every power but the power of telepathy. Actually, I was glad. I didn't want him to hear my senseless inner babble.

Farid's eyes were glazed as he scanned over the cave drawings. The one with the amulets stood out above all the others with its deep red stain and golden lines.

"Whenever you're ready," Calliel said softly.

Farid came to stand beside me. His presence was a huge comfort. It almost stifled the longing I had for Ammun . . . almost. That longing would never completely disappear. It was now a part of me forever, but I was going to learn to ignore it. I would shove it into a deep, dark corner, and now was as good a time as any to start.

Calliel swept me up in a heartfelt bear hug. Her watering eyes left a warm dampness behind on my cheeks. Her sadness was infectious. I felt the tiny droplets falling from my eyes as well. Rhiya reached over to hug me too.

Dearg was next. "I will miss you lots and lots," he grumbled. His stone expression revealed no sincerity to emphasize what he had said, but I knew he truly meant it.

"I will miss you too," I replied, wiping the tears from my eyes. I hated crying, but I found that I couldn't help it anymore.

"I'll come visit because I'm traveler. I'm the only creature that can come visit," he said proudly.

"I'd like that," I said. I wasn't sure how Dearg could visit after the borders were locked, but as always, I was sure he knew more than I did. Dearg could be irritating—he could be ignorant—but I loved him as he was, and I knew he wasn't a liar.

Over his shoulders I caught sight of Ammun's face. It was hard to make out his expression. He stood in darkness, wallowing in the shadows. His arms were crossed over his chest. I wished I knew what he was thinking. Would he think about me when I was gone?

I pulled away from Calliel and walked slowly toward him. I willed him to turn his face up and look at me. I thought he would never do it, but he did . . . eventually. He spoke before I even had a chance to move my lips.

"I'm sorry," he said.

I wasn't expecting that.

Those were my words. I meant to say them, but he had beaten me to it, and now, I had nothing left to say because it wasn't okay. I didn't want to forgive him. I was afraid that if I spoke I would burst into tears, so I simply nodded. My throat felt dry and my eyes stung, but it was nothing compared to the mix of emotions I felt inside.

Ammun raised his hand as if he meant to brush away the stray wisps of hair on my face, but he held back. He forced his hand back down to his side. "Goodbye, Isra," he said finally. His voice was soft and kind. It would have been soothing had the words been different.

I knew in that moment that it was settled. He chose being an angel over me, and I chose Earth over him. He held my gaze for less than a second before dropping his head again. There was something else he had wanted to say, and I wish I knew what it was. I gave him a questioning look, but he shook his head. Whatever it was, he had no intention of sharing it with me.

Reluctantly, I pulled away from him and took my place beside Farid. Our palms touched and he entwined his fingers into mine. He radiated a strong sense of security and safety. Right now, I felt like he would never have hurt me, even when the Abaddon ordered him to kill me. He had already made the decision . . . maybe seconds, maybe minutes, or maybe hours before. I wanted to believe that he had never meant to hurt me.

I raised my amulet, and Farid gave me an encouraging glance. He smiled and copied my movement, holding the amulet away from his body in his left hand. Together, we touched the cave drawings with our hands and then the amulets. They trembled with a heavy vibration, so strong that it could be powerfully heard as well as seen. The throbbing increased until the amulets burst into the fierce flickering of flames. Their orange tips licked our hands, but there was no pain. None at all. The fire leaped like an animal, crouching low, and then emerging to its full height. It was an elegant, agile animal that had so completely captured our attention we could no longer turn away. We stared at it, mesmerized.

When it was finally done showing off, it formed the rectangular shape of a doorway. I knew that the moment I stepped through that doorway—this world; Calliel, Rhiya, Ammun—it would all be nothing but a memory fading with time. But I had to let go. I had to give it all up. This wasn't my world. I didn't belong here. I belonged on Earth with my sister.

I allowed Farid to pull me through. I went back to where I belonged. My home. Earth would *always* be my home. I was lucky to have been able to catch a glimpse of Zarcane, but that was all it was meant to be. A glimpse, and nothing more. Yes, it was beautiful, captivating. It was a place created out of the fabrics of my dreams. A place I thought I would only *see* in my dreams. I had completed my job as the Keeper and now, it was time to leave. I forced myself not to turn around and glance at Ammun, however much I wanted to. I needed to forget about him.

"Goodbye," I whispered.

Thirty-Nine

Isra

"Isra! Isra, wake up!" Zaffirah jolted me out of my sleep. I felt the direct burn as my shocked retinas adjusted to the brightly lit room. Thoughts nibbled around the edges of my brain, forbidding me to go back to sleep. Thoughts of Ammun and Zarcane. It took me a moment to see through the disorientation. I was in the chair next to Zaffirah's bed, in the hospital. Calliel and Rhiya hadn't returned.

"I found this." Zaffirah held up a piece of paper. It was a note. I scanned over it.

Dear Zaffirah & Isra,

Thank you for everything that you have done for us. Isra, you were one of the most honest and virtuous Keepers that I have encountered in my time. Just like your mother. She would have been proud. Zaffirah, love her. Treasure her like she does you. I know that once I enter Zarcane, I shall not return. If you, however, survive what waits for us there, I wish you both the very bes,t and I hope you know that our home will always be open to you and your friends.

Love,
Calliel

"I guess that's where we're staying, then?" Zaffirah asked.

I nodded. "Looks like it," I replied. I avoided stating the fact that we really had nowhere else to go. Wandering the streets was out of the question. I wasn't putting Zaffirah in that kind of danger ever again. Certainly not by choice.

"Count me in, too."

Farid rested his elbow on the doorway, grinning widely. His breathing was heavy and his hair, disheveled. He looked like he had been running.

"Don't you already have a home? A family to take care of?" I asked.

"They didn't even notice I was gone. They don't care."

I nodded in understanding. Calliel's house was way too big for just Zaffirah and me. It would be a comfort having Farid around to share it.

"Well, you look healthy enough to run laps around a soccer field, so are we allowed to leave?" he asked Zaffirah.

She smiled defiantly. "The doctors don't have to know."

Farid raised his eyebrows and looked at me questioningly.

"If anyone has any brilliant ideas about getting out of here without the doctors knowing, please do share. I don't have the money to pay for however much this fancy hospital costs."

Silence. No one said a word. The lines on Farid's face creased as he sank deeper into his thoughts. Zaffirah cocked her head to one side and played with a loose strand of her hair. I touched the amulet around my neck, absently.

"We'll walk out. We'll just casually walk out, and no one will notice us," I said finally.

"Yes, that is our only option," Farid agreed.

So that's what we did. We simply walked out of the hospital, and no one bothered to stop us. Doctors and nurses were a blur of white, rushing to take care of their patients. They didn't have the least bit of time for three completely capable, healthy looking people that had just maybe purposely forgotten to pay their bills.

It didn't take too long for us to walk to Calliel's larger-than-a-cottage-but-smaller-than-a-mansion home. It was as welcoming as I remembered it. Maybe even more so, now that we really had nowhere else to go, and it was deprived of an owner.

"What? I don't see anything." Farid rubbed his eyes.

"Me neither," Zaffirah said.

"Are you kidding? It's right there . . . oh, wait." I remembered Rhiya's instructions when she had first brought me to her home. That now seemed so long ago. What had she called the disguise? Glamour, I think it was.

"The house is there, you just can't see it, yet. Turn to the right, then left . . ." I tried to remember the rest. "And, um . . . blink twice. I think that's it . . ."

They looked at me like I had lost my mind. I remembered that look on my face, and the hesitance with which I had proceeded to do as Rhiya had said. "Come on, guys. What happened to the trust?"

"And you promise you're not doing this just to laugh at us?" Farid asked.

"Guess you'll have to try it and see," I replied. "Don't worry, we've got all day. We've all slept outside before . . . but just imagine the soft, comfy, warm beds."

That seemed to have more of an effect on them than anything I had said before. Instantly, their heads were twisting and their eyelids rapidly falling. I knew from the look of awe on their faces that they could now see the house.

"Do you have the keys?" Zaffirah and Farid asked together.

I shook my head and before they had time to react, I

walked over to the door and twisted the golden knob. "You don't need keys for a house that no one knows *how* to see."

Farid shrugged. "Well, I guess that makes sense."

He entered behind me, followed closely by Zaffirah. I knew that the house we were in was probably the kind of house they had only ever seen in pictures. Now, the pictures had turned into a pleasant reality.

"Isra, when I was . . . you know, in a coma . . . did you stay here?" Zaffirah asked. Her eyes were gulping in the heavy wooden furniture and the paint-covered walls. They were luxuries that only the affluents could afford. Luxuries that she probably thought we would never be allowed to touch, let alone indulge in.

"Is this real?" Farid said softly.

I nodded. "Rhiya found me on the streets. I was looking for you, Zaffirah. She said she could help me, and I was getting desperate."

"I'm glad she found you," Zaffirah said finally, when she was done staring at a painting of a horse. I hadn't noticed that painting before. The white horse was galloping in a field that was green, like Farid's eyes.

"Me too. Come. I have to show you the rooms upstairs!"

"Yes!" Farid exclaimed.

"Wait. *There's an upstairs?*" Zaffirah cried incredulously. The smile on her face was huge now. I didn't think that there was anything in the world that could bring her down. I loved seeing her like that. It made *me* smile. I hadn't seen her this happy since my father . . . . I shook the thought away, not wanting to ruin the moment. She was happy, and that was all that mattered.

I pushed open the door of the first room on the left of the staircase. It was the room that I had stayed in. I noticed that everything was exactly as I had left it. I had a feeling that no one had been in here since I had left, except . . . . I walked toward a hump on the bed.

"Isra, what is it?" Farid asked. He came to stand beside me and peered at the bulging duvet.

"It's probably just a pillow or something."

"Pillows don't breathe." Zaffirah pointed, and I noticed the bulge's rising and falling chest.

"Stop worrying. I'm sure it's nothing," I said.

Farid walked around the bed and grabbed the metal lamp from the side table. Then carefully, with his forefinger and thumb, he lowered the blanket.

"Boo! I missed you! I couldn't stay without you!"

Dearg leaped off the bed and jumped into my arms. Farid lowered the lamp, jaw hanging.

"Wasn't he supposed to stay . . . in Zarcane?"

Dearg shook his head stubbornly. "Corom went to Zarcane so I stay here!"

"Who's Corom?" Farid asked.

"He was the traveler that was here with Calliel. He was a creature like Dearg. I guess they switched places . . . or something," I murmured.

Dearg nodded quickly, his bulging yellow eyes wide.

Fourty

Isra

Zaffirah curled into bed that night, and Farid sat beside her, telling her a story about a crippled dragon, a lonely man, and a beautiful girl. Zaffirah was asleep before he even got to the end. I shut the lights off, and we both walked out of the room.

"It was a good story," I complimented.

"Oh. Thanks," Farid mumbled.

"I have a question though. What happens to the drag- on?" I asked, filling two mugs with the warm tea I had found in a cupboard in the kitchen. We sat down on Calliel's huge, brown table.

"What do you mean?" Farid countered.

"Well, did he ever get to fly again?"

He shrugged. "Maya asked the same thing. It's just a story," he reflected, looking away from me.

I didn't know what to say, so I said nothing. I had never been very good at comforting anyone. Instead, I passed him the mug of tea and watched him slowly take a sip.

"Too sweet," he yelped, puckering his lips and pushing the mug away.

"Sorry," I mumbled. "I should have warned you. I might have gone a little crazy with the sugar."

He waved off my apology and looked at me wearily. Though he no longer sported the deep knife wound, he still looked pale enough that I could easily believe that just hours ago, he had been grievously injured. He put up a good show for Zaffirah, making jokes and telling stories. Despite his faults, of which there were many, he would always know how to put a smile on any child's face. I was extremely glad for that. He would be the perfect piece to complete our broken family. All Zaffirah would know about his is that he helped me defeat the Abaddon. How we got there would be a story for another time.

"I can't believe it's over," he murmured. "All we have left is a damn good tale to tell, and this." He pulled the amulet from his pocket and laid it on the table.

"A tale no one but the next Keepers will believe," I added, setting my amulet beside his. The two amulets now looked so ordinary. The color I'd once thought so special was now simply a muddy red. I could hardly believe they were the keys to a land as old as Adam and Eve, with creatures from only our imaginations.

"So, do we just put them away somewhere safe until these new Keepers come along?" Farid asked.

"I guess so." I shrugged.

We put the amulets in a cardboard box and pried one of the floorboards open. Farid lowered the box into the dark hole, and I put the floorboard back in place. That's where the amulets would stay, collecting dust and becoming a home to a million spiders. They would be like dead bodies, awaiting their resurrection by the new Keepers, while Farid and I would continue our lives and forget the land that we had temporarily been so completely a part of. We would live normal lives and convince ourselves that everything we had seen was not just a dream, but a dream in another lifetime in an alternate universe so very far away. We would no longer be the Keepers of Eden, but simply Isra and Farid, born and brought up in a filthy slum in Islamabad. The question was, can you really force yourself to forget tremors of the past, or is it all just a convincing game of pretense?

Epilogue

D awn; the sun's first light fell upon the market. Men, groggy with sleep in their eyes, had begun setting up their stalls, awaiting the first customers that daylight would bring their way. Beggars offered to help for a small coin, and a few women walked around, eyeing things in carts that had already been put on display.

A wingless insect crawled up the trouser leg of a boy, and he shook it off. The boy rolled his arms, trying to release the pain that ran in two slanted lines across his back.

He stopped by a woman selling flowers and picked up a rose. The woman named her price, and the boy considered it. He almost pulled out the silver coins in his pocket, but he thought better of it and put the flower back in its place. The seller yelled out a lower price, trying to convince the boy to come back, but it was too late. He had already walked away and exchanged those coins for an apple.

The boy then walked quickly through the market. The more he thought about where he wanted to go, the harder the frown on his face became. He squeezed his eyelids shut and tried to calm the storm swirling inside him. He quickened his pace and smacked head on into someone else. A green-eyed boy with a box of wooden carvings. He was here to sell them off to anyone who would take them, at a price much lower than they probably deserved. But that didn't matter. For once in his life, he wasn't desperate for money. He was perfectly content.

"Ammun," Farid gasped out and dropped the box. The mini wooden statues spilled out in a wave of browns. Ants crawled over them, inspecting them for morsels of food that they could take back with them.

Ammun went to the ground and brushed off the insects. He put the sculptures back in the box they had fallen out of and held out the box to Farid as an offering, but Farid was still too shocked to move.

"You came back," he breathed out finally.

"I did," Ammun said simply. He had nothing more to say on the matter. At least, nothing more to say to Farid.

About Anoosha

Anoosha Lalani has always had an insatiable desire to escape reality. It was a childhood trait that never seemed to fade out. If Anoosha were to make one wish, it would be to have wings to journey off the face of this planet and into the worlds of her stories.

When she's not writing, you may find Anoosha attending high school in Singapore. Having moved around so much, she has had the wonderful opportunity to be exposed to a vibrant range of cultures, which often seem to find their way into her stories. Anoosha was born in Pakistan, the setting of her most recent novel, *The Keepers*.

Acknowledgements

It takes almost a small village to create a book. I might be author of this story but I'm also only one member of that village it took to complete the book that you currently have before you. For that reason I would like to thank the following people for touching my book in their own special way.

My parents, for keeping me grounded when my head flew a little too high in the clouds. Thank you for making sure I graduated and made it to a university.

My friends, both writers and not, for supporting me

and my writing in every possible way. I love the way you guys feigned immense interest in everything I had to say about my dear Isra and Farid.

My editor, **Cait Spivey**, for having the patience to guide me through cutting away all the rough edges my story once contained. Not only did my book come out better because of her, but her invaluable advice also allowed me to vastly improve the way I write.

And finally to the rest of the gang at **REUTS**, **Ashley**, **Kisa**, **Summer** and **Tiffany**, thank you for breathing life into the perfect picture in my head.

CPSIA information can be obtained
at www.ICGtesting.com
Printed in the USA
LVOW11s1239261217
560821LV00001B/96/P